Jordyn's Choice

Jordyn's Choice

By Blake Channels

Blossom Cove Publishing

Cover art by swissmediavision.

Cover design by J. Brown.

Edited by Melissa Schab.

Published 2021

ISBN: 978-0-9998142-4-6

Published by Blossom Cove Publishing.

To find out more about the author and available books, visit blakechannels.com.

To Melissa,

For being my cherished sister, editor, publicist – and self-proclaimed biggest fan.

Chapter One

Three minutes. Precisely the amount of time before Jordyn Reilly would know if her life would be changed forever. It should seem an insignificant amount of time. But the second hand on the clock ticked away at an agonizing pace as she gazed out the window of her modest log home, doing her best to endure the small span of eternity she was being forced to wait. But Jordyn's frown transformed into a smile as she admired the way the snow fell on her sleepy little town. From her hilltop view she watched in awe as a brilliant blanket of white settled over the rooftops below. Admired the warm glow of the porchlights against the early morning sky while the sun slumbered behind the mountain peaks.

At its pinnacle, the small town of Sugarcreek, Colorado had been a booming mining town with a prosperous sugar mill that had kept most of the townsfolk employed. Now, with the mill closed, the local economy relied on tourism to continue to thrive. But thrive it did.

Loaded with small-town charm, vacationers flocked to Sugarcreek like moths to a flame—drawn to the allure of hiking, kayaking, fishing, and Miss Betsy's homemade pies. Truth be told Miss Betsy had retired a decade earlier and her beloved pies were now baked by loyal employees entrusted with the family recipe (a closely guarded secret amongst the locals). Sugarcreek's colder months promised sledding and a winter wonderland which provided a tranquil backdrop for tourists to browse local shops in search of unique holiday gifts. The town hosted an annual Christmas tree lighting ceremony complete with a parade, live music, and festive activities for kids and adults alike. That time of year the streets were thick with tourists, musicians, and the smell of hot spiced cider and kettle corn.

Jordyn had woken up early that morning to apply a final coat of varnish to the custom piece she'd designed for the lobby of *Donna's Bed and Breakfast*. The hand-carved bench had taken longer than she'd anticipated, but it had turned out beautiful. She was confident Donna would agree.

While the varnish dried, she indulged in a cup of peppermint tea by the fireplace and waited impatiently for the clock to read 7:04. She sipped the tea with reverence, enjoying the view and the company of a roaring fire as she rested a hand on her flat belly and let herself dream about the prospect of being a mother. Would the baby have her chestnut hair, or would it be a bit lighter like Brody's? Perhaps the baby would have Brody's chocolate brown eyes—though she wouldn't mind them being an emerald green like hers.

The timer on her phone went off, interrupting her drifting thoughts and the tranquil setting. With eager anticipation, she silenced the timer and hurried to the bathroom. All smiles, and heart hammering in her chest, she plucked the pregnancy test from the bathroom counter, mentally preparing to celebrate the expected outcome. But her good mood fizzled and her face fell as she stared in disbelief and disappointment at yet another negative test result.

This time she'd been so sure. It was a few days before she was due for her monthly cycle. But sore breasts. A fluttering in her belly she had been certain was proof of an early pregnancy. Choking back tears, she buried the test stick and its unwelcome result in the bottom of the bathroom trash can—filled with regret she couldn't bury her feelings with the same ease.

Shuffling to the sink, she stared at her paled reflection in the mirror. It was as if she was staring into the face of her pain. She sucked in her breath as insurmountable disappointment ripped through her. She wondered how she could endure yet another crushing letdown. She was still young, she reminded herself. But not as young as she once was. Her despair gave way to anger.

It's not fair, she told her reflection. Then, after a bout of internal deliberation where she weighed the responsibilities of running her store against the heaviness of her heart, she decided against going into work.

"You win," she whispered in agony to the crestfallen face in the mirror, temporarily giving into her sorrow and deciding to take a day for herself.

She called her friend and assistant manager, Hailie, to ask if she could cover for her at the store. She knew Saturdays at *Homespun Goodness* were typically hectic but couldn't bring herself to smile for her customers when all she wanted to do was curl up in a ball and cry. Fortunately, she had only one interior design consultation she'd need to make that day.

When Hailie received Jordyn's phone call, she agreed without hesitation. "Happy to cover," she said cheerily. Then, after a pause she asked, "Is everything okay?" It was unlike her friend to blow off work at her beloved store on such short notice. Especially on a Saturday so close to the holidays.

"Oh everything's fine, I just have some things to take care of," Jordyn said vaguely. "I can handle the consult if you can manage the store today."

Although Jordyn tried to remain upbeat, Hailie caught the hint of melancholy in her friend's tone. Since Jordyn also didn't offer any real explanation for needing to take the day off, Hailie suspected she knew what was wrong. She was one of the few people Jordyn had confided in about trying to have a baby. The pain in her friend's tone was unmistakable, no matter how hard she tried to mask it.

"I'm happy to do it," she repeated, feeling helpless and wishing there were more she could do for her friend. When Hailie had moved to town three years earlier, Jordyn had taken her under her wing, offering her a job at *Homespun Goodness* and, more importantly, a devoted friendship. Small towns didn't always embrace strangers. There was a stigma that if you didn't grow up there, you couldn't be trusted. Or that if you moved to a small town, you were running away from something. And Hailie's punk rock pink pixie cut may have been a turnoff for some. But Jordyn had made her feel welcome from the start and didn't pry into her reasons for coming to Sugarcreek until she was ready to reveal them.

Jordyn arrived at Masters Manor a few minutes early, anxious to get the appointment out of the way. An elaborate, hand-carved wooden sign above an iron gate marked the entrance to the regal estate that looked more like a ski lodge than a house. She passed through the open gate and pulled to the front of the circle drive. It was a grand place surrounded by hundreds of acres of pastureland, cattle, and a speckling of barns and other outbuildings. A stream ran the length of the property, bordered by Blue Spruce trees and the occasional Chokecherry shrub. The snow-covered mountain tops above made a majestic backdrop.

The hotel-sized house was familiar to Jordyn. She'd had the pleasure of decorating many of its fine rooms. She was always paid a handsome commission, but at the end of the day, it felt like she was playing house. Designing pieces she couldn't keep. Ordering furniture she herself could never afford. She was proud of the house she shared with Brody, and her personal touches that had transformed it into a home. But lately each job at Masters Manor made her feel more dissatisfied, and Jordyn was both surprised and ashamed by her shallowness.

As she clambered out of the car, the chill in the air took her breath away. She should have braced herself for the biting wind, she supposed, but with the brilliant way the sun sparkled off the layers of freshly packed snow, sometimes she forgot that with all that dazzling white came an unforgiving cold.

Tucking her head low to avoid the sting of the relentless wind, she made her way to the front entrance. Ignoring the ornate doorbell she knew would play a cheery Christmas song she wasn't in the mood for, Jordyn knocked instead. As she waited, she twisted her engagement ring around her finger, feeling like a fraud.

A man dressed in crisp black slacks and a white, button-up shirt opened the front door to her.

"Hello, Mr. Davis." Jordyn wasn't precisely sure what the man's job title was, but she supposed he could be described as a modern-day butler.

"Ms. Reilly, right this way." He politely motioned her through the front door.

Jordyn smiled in response to the man's unrelenting formalities, regardless of how often they'd been introduced. He never offered up his first name, nor did he greet Jordyn by her given name despite her reassurance that he was welcome to do so. Mr. Davis took her coat and gloves and she allowed herself to be led through the foyer and into the living room where Molly was seated on the sofa with a cup of tea. He offered Jordyn a cup and a seat, both of which she politely declined, then excused himself from the room.

Molly set down her tea, stood to her feet, and crossed the room to meet Jordyn, offering her a warm embrace. Jordyn felt herself stiffen in response.

"You look radiant," Molly said, seemingly unaware of Jordyn's awkward response to the hug.

Her eyes widened in surprise. "Thank you, as do you," she said, returning the unexpected compliment. Then, trying to keep her tone light and friendly, she asked, "So, what decorating challenge do you have for me this time?"

It wasn't that she didn't like Molly. Other than the fact her married name—Molly Masters—had the ring of a talk-show host, what was not to like? She was sweet, warm, and giving. Attractive, with a generous mouth and lean build. Her eyebrows were perhaps a bit thinner than was fashionable in recent years. But she was pretty, nonetheless.

The two had tolerated each other fine their final two years in high school. More than that—one could argue they'd been friends. Both active in school functions and fundraisers. Both members of the cheerleading squad. Of course Molly Masters had been Molly Hauser back then. She'd moved with her family from Austin, Texas to Sugarcreek, Colorado her junior year. Straight away the boys had taken to her Texas accent and long, auburn hair.

Molly wore her hair shorter now and bleached it to an almost platinum blonde. She had a deep tan despite the approaching winter. It was the kind of sun-kissed glow one could only get that time of year at *Kay's Sun Spa*, the tannery downtown. It was a popular spot for local housewives and tourists alike. Jordyn suspected the tan skin and light hair color were Kane's preferences. Molly's reddish-brown hair color was gone, along with her Texas accent.

As much as Jordyn hated to admit it to herself, jealousy was the likely culprit keeping the two women from being friends. Jealousy on Jordyn's part, that is. It was unlikely Molly had a jealous bone in her lean and pampered southern body.

"A new nursery," Molly announced proudly, answering Jordyn's question as she patted her flat tummy.

Jordyn's plastered smile fell from her face. Molly's words were like a punch to the gut. An affirmation that others could easily attain the beautiful things in life that for her seemed out of reach. An actual marriage instead of a sham engagement to taper the smalltown gossip that was inevitable when two people lived together out of wedlock. Precious children. She and Brody had been trying for a baby. Trying for two years, unbeknownst to most. Jordyn had been so convinced she'd wanted a house full of kids. She'd never paused to consider she might not be able to have even one. And here was Molly, proudly expecting her third child while her two, perfect children—a boy and a girl—played quietly in the next room.

Smarting from the news, Jordyn wanted to ask if the pregnancy meant Molly would have to give up her precious tanning bed sessions. But with her smile set back in place, she offered her congratulations instead. Then, with as much enthusiasm as she could muster, she asked, "Boy or girl?"

Molly glowed as she stroked her invisible baby bump. "We want it to be a surprise this time."

She felt another pang of jealousy at hearing the word *we*. Jordyn had dated Kane Masters in high school. The relationship had started halfway through her sophomore year and had lasted until graduation. He'd been charming, good-looking—not to mention his father had owned the biggest cattle ranch in the county, which Kane was set to inherit, making him the biggest catch in town. But Jordyn was drawn to the city life, and she'd broken things off with him to pursue her dreams of living in New York. By the time she'd returned to Sugarcreek, Kane had married Molly and the couple was expecting their first child.

Jordyn hadn't minded at first. Shortly after moving back to Sugarcreek, she'd met Brody while attending a fundraiser at the animal shelter. At the time she'd been a career-seeking college student who had temporarily returned to her hometown to make funeral arrangements for her parents and settle their estate. She'd been devastated by their deaths and the gaping hole it left in her life. Brody had walked into the shelter carrying an injured puppy and she'd fallen head over heels—instantly forgetting her plans to return to New York as she found herself getting lost in his soft, brown eyes. And while she'd never get over losing her parents, he'd lovingly and patiently helped her through the most tragic experience of her life. Picking up the shattered pieces she'd been too heartbroken to gather up herself.

A loud shriek sounded from the next room, penetrating her thoughts.

"Mommy, Mommy, Levi hit me," little Stephanie-Ann squealed as she ran into the room and wrapped her pudgy arms around her mother's leg. Levi ran in after her, hollering and waving a plastic hammer in the air. The two children looked like miniature versions of Kane as they wreaked havoc in the formerly peaceful living room. Dark hair. Big, soulful eyes. Strikingly attractive.

Molly looked up sharply. "Now, Levi, where did you learn to behave like that?" Jordyn noticed a hint of the Texas accent return.

Levi glowered at his mother, as if he had something he wanted to say, but he remained quiet.

"Now apologize to your sister."

"I'm sorry, Stephanie-Ann," he spat out but his blue eyes remained clouded in anger.

"Look your sister in the eye and say it like you mean it."

With a contrite expression, Levi mumbled a more heartfelt apology, then gave his sister a hug.

Molly straightened the collar on her daughter's dress and smoothed her son's dark, wavy hair. "There. Now go play," she told them both.

As if on cue, Tiffany, the nanny and housekeeper, bustled in to herd the children from the room. The young, petite blonde looked frazzled and offered a quick apology about being distracted. Her excuse was met with a tight smile from Molly. While Jordyn had always been impressed by Mr. Davis, to her Tiffany had always seemed a bit flighty. She suspected it was Molly's patient and forgiving nature that kept the housekeeper employed.

Once the children left the room, Molly turned back to Jordyn and said, "Boys will be boys I guess." She looked embarrassed and her tone was a bit melancholy. Then, as quickly as it had come, her downcast expression faded and her cheerful demeanor returned.

"So, what room is to be the new nursery?" Jordyn asked, trying to move things along.

"The reading room. Turns out none of us are avid readers."

Jordyn nodded but felt a twinge of disappointment. She loved the reading room. It was one of her first interior design jobs at Masters Manor and perhaps the most distinctive room in the house. It boasted a comfy sofa chair and ottoman atop a plush, bohemian style rug. The walls were lined with floor to ceiling bookshelves. The impressive assortment of books, with their variety of genres and beautiful covers, was like a work of art. She had personally picked out every book that lined the solid wooden shelves and was shocked at how easily Molly could dismiss such a masterpiece.

Forcing a smile, Jordyn said, "Reading room it is." At first, she pondered whether Molly might let her keep some of the books she had worked so hard to procure and which Molly was so quick to discard. Then she cleared her throat, along with her self-serving thoughts, and tried to channel some creative enthusiasm.

"Have you thought about a color scheme?"

"I was thinking soft grays and creams."

This prompted another nod of artificial enthusiasm. *Boring*. But the expression of pride on her client's face softened Jordyn's response. As not to hurt Molly's feelings, she paused, considering her word choice.

"That would work well for either a boy or a girl." Her brow knitted in concentration. "We may be able to add pops of some more vibrant colors to make sure it doesn't look too starchy or cold." *Or like an asylum*, she thought to herself, annoyed Molly didn't just find out the sex of the baby so she could take more liberties with the color palette.

She silently surveyed the room, quietly committing to memory every detail of the lovely space she'd soon have to dismantle. Then she pulled out her sketchbook and began to outline the room—imagining it as a blank canvas. She measured the room's dimensions and jotted them down. This got the creative juices flowing. Setting aside her reservations, she began to sketch fresh ideas for a nursery.

"Well, I'll leave you to it," Molly said, sensing she was hindering the process.

Jordyn nodded but didn't look up from her drawings. As her fingers gripped the pencil, she let her imagination run away with her. In the far corner of the room would be a dresser with a changing table on top. She envisioned a crib with a mobile of gray, fluffy elephants circling overhead. She could still make use of one of the walls of shelves.

The current selection of novels would be replaced by children's books, stuffed animals, and decorative bins to hold smaller items like diapers, building blocks, and teething rings. The reading room offered a fireplace, so she sketched a cozy rocking chair next to it. She smiled to herself as the room started to take shape. A simple, hand-painted mural on the wall opposite the window. A plush rug to add some texture.

"Can I get you some hot cocoa?" Molly's voice disrupted the silence.

Jordyn jumped at the unexpected interruption.

"I'm so sorry. I didn't mean to startle you."

"That's alright. I was just finishing up." She snapped her sketchbook shut and smiled up at her client. Without realizing it, she studied her. Despite spending most of her time at home, Molly was decked out in a white pantsuit with a pink, silk chamise. Jordyn had also worn a suit that day. It was her favorite navy-blue pinstripe skirt suit. But next to Molly and her designer label clothing, the outfit that normally made her feel so confident now felt like exactly what it was. A cheap suit.

"I'll work up a simulation on the computer and get it over to you in a day or two if that works."

"Absolutely."

"Will I see you at the upcoming bake sale?" Jordyn asked, making friendly conversation, and doing her best to ignore the way Molly's hand kept returning to her belly to rest protectively over the invisible bump.

"Wouldn't miss it. Kane volunteered to manage the popcorn stand," she announced proudly.

"Wonderful, then I'll see you both there." She could tell her cheery tone sounded forced. She made her retreat, leaving Molly and the lavish mansion behind, along with two children and the life Jordyn realized could have been hers.

Chapter Two

Brody Kingston removed his brown felt sheriff's hat and set it on the kitchen counter. He raked his fingers through his thick, sandy blonde hair and exhaled deeply. He felt drained as he rummaged through the refrigerator for a carton of milk. He poured himself a generous glass, then lifted the glass from the countertop. Studying its contents, he wished it were a cold beer instead. But he refused to use drinking as a coping mechanism. As a cop, he'd seen far too many times where that could lead.

Usually known for his ramrod posture and neat, tidy uniform, at present his broad shoulders stooped ever so slightly. His shirt was untucked and he unbuttoned the top two buttons before draining his glass of milk.

When Jordyn padded into the kitchen, Brody was too preoccupied by the day's events to appreciate the new, black negligée she wore beneath her open silk robe. Just as he was too preoccupied to notice her drawn expression or the pained look in her eyes.

"Rough day?" Jordyn asked him, though she suspected she already knew the answer. There was no mistaking the worried looked etched on his handsome face. His eyes, usually so soft and full of compassion, were dark and broody.

He nodded but didn't offer anything further. For a small town, Sugarcreek was starting to see more than its fair share of crime. The harsh winters led to drinking, which often led to increased petty crime and domestic violence. But lately it was more than that. Drugs and prostitution were seeping into the town he loved, and as sheriff, he felt personally responsible. Crime patterns were far too sophisticated to be random. No, he suspected organized crime backed by someone powerful. Someone with unlimited funds. Funds that kept growing alongside the corruption.

Jordyn walked over to him, circled her arms around his neck, and planted a kiss on his cheek. "Sorry about your day." Her tone was flat and Brody noticed her sullen mood for the first time.

"Busy day at work?" he asked hesitantly. He cupped her chin in his hand, gently forcing her to meet his gaze. His brown eyes softened and narrowed in concern as he fought to interpret her somber expression. He hoped some of the unsavory characters creeping into his town weren't bothering her at the store. He'd considered warning her to take extra precautions but after careful deliberation, had decided he didn't want to worry her. He'd been having one of his men conduct extra patrols instead.

Jordyn thought about not mentioning that she'd taken the day off but figured he'd find out eventually. "Actually, I had Hailie cover for me at the store today. I needed the break."

"Okay, then...?" he gently prodded.

"I did have an appointment with Molly Masters."

Brody stiffened. "Was Kane there?" The local sheriff didn't dislike many people in his town, but he loathed Kane. He had his reasons—some more justified than others. And upon learning that Kane planned to run for mayor next term, he had one more reason to dislike the man he felt already had too much influence over Sugarcreek.

"Nope. Just Molly and her two children... Oh, and the baby she announced they have on the way." Her voice broke. She tried to appear stoic but her tears betrayed her and she stood powerless as they escaped and seeped down her soft cheeks.

"Oh, babe, I'm so sorry." Brody wrapped her in his arms and she buried her face into his chest. He patted her chestnut hair as she cried softly, soaking the front of his starched, khaki green shirt.

She could tell he'd also had a rough day and hadn't planned to burden him with her troubles. But once the dam of emotions broke, the words spilled out alongside her tears. "And on top of that," she said through her grief, "I took a pregnancy test today and it came back negative."

Brody hugged her tighter as regret settled in his gut. He wanted a baby as much as she did. It killed him that he couldn't give Jordyn what she wanted most. And it was a delicate dance to convey his disappointment without making the woman he loved feel even worse. He knew to outsiders it might seem strange, starting a family without being married. But neither he nor Jordyn always acted conventionally. "We'll try again, sweetheart."

She stepped back and wiped her tears with the back of her hand. Then she offered him the faintest smile. "Well, I thought maybe…" Biting her lower lip, she looked down at her bare legs, then stared expectantly into Brody's soft, brown eyes.

His breath hitched and he grinned wolfishly, noticing the negligée for the first time and the way it clung to Jordyn's curvy hips and toned thighs. He pushed back her robe, appreciating how striking the black lace of her nightgown looked against her creamy skin. He felt shame he hadn't noticed until now. He'd always considered himself lucky to be with Jordyn and never wanted her to think she was being taken for granted. He loved her. She'd rescued him in so many ways.

He peered into her glistening green eyes, wiped away her tears, then pressed his lips to hers. As he wrapped his strong arms around her, he navigated their bodies towards the kitchen counter. With painstaking care and a certain degree of skill, he kept his lips and body pressed firmly against hers as he swiped a bottle of red from the wine rack behind her and rummaged in the kitchen drawer for a bottle opener.

"Wine for dinner?" Jordyn asked, coming up for air.

Brody grinned, taking in by the adorable flush on her cheeks. "I'm in if you are."

She nodded and her body hummed with passion. "Bring the handcuffs," she teased.

They tore at each other's clothes as they raced towards the bedroom. When Jordyn's negligée hit the floor, their worries were temporarily forgotten. There was only room for desire.

Chapter Three

There were two churches in Sugarcreek. Both well attended. Neither claimed a specific religion but they were affectionately referred to as the *new age* church and the *old school* church. Despite her young age, Jordyn preferred the *old school* church with its traditional ideals and classic hymnals. The *new age* church was a bit too trendy for her taste. But it did offer an eleven o'clock sermon, often making it the choice by default. Sunday was the one day a week she allowed herself to sleep in.

"You coming with me today?" she asked Brody, who laid lazily beside her, one bare leg over hers and a muscular arm draped over her naked torso.

Brody groaned. He would like nothing more than to just lie in bed with her. "Isn't there a later service?"

"Eleven *is* the later service," she reminded him with a smirk.

"We could stay in bed and, you know, try again." He trailed his index finger over Jordyn's bare thigh, admiring how serene she looked and the contrast of her chestnut hair splayed across the white cotton sheets.

She shivered with pleasure at his touch, then, reminding herself she was not one to miss Sunday service, she hit him playfully on the shoulder. "Have you no shame?"

Brody brushed her cheek with the back of his hand. "Not when it comes to you."

Despite his misgivings, he attended church for two reasons. One being that, as the local sheriff, it was expected of him. The people of Sugarcreek felt more comfortable entrusting their safety to a *God-fearing man*. But the main reason he went was because it made Jordyn happy. She had faith like nobody he'd ever met and he knew how important it was to her to share it with him.

It wasn't that he wasn't a believer. It was more that he harbored bitterness in his heart. Bitterness that, despite how hard he tried, was directed towards God. His anger began when he lost his father at fifteen but took a turn for the worst after his wife was murdered. Born and raised in San Francisco, he'd remained there to study criminology at San Francisco State University. After graduating with a degree in Criminal Justice, he joined the San Francisco Police Department and married Paige, his best friend and high school sweetheart.

He'd been on duty the night he'd gotten the call that she'd been found shot in an alley. An apparent mugging while she was walking back to her car with an armful of groceries. His first love. Her precious life snuffed out for a wedding band, gold necklace, and an insignificant amount of cash. Tossed away like trash.

Her death was the reason he'd come to Sugarcreek. The open deputy position gave him the chance to leave his metropolitan lifestyle behind and start over in a quiet town. But Jordyn had been the reason he'd stayed. He'd thought he'd never love again after Paige, but she'd quickly proved him wrong. Passionate, caring, talented, beautiful. He'd fallen hard for her. And once Sheriff Lampson retired, Brody was elected for the job—running unopposed. The town was enamored with his education and big-city experience.

The sermon went longer than usual. Reverend Jacobs prattled on, seemingly entranced by the sound of his own voice. He covered everything. The power of forgiveness. Giving until it hurt. Having a servant's heart. When Brody shifted uncomfortably on the hard, wooden pew, Jordyn poked him playfully in the ribs. Then she took his hand in hers and gave it a gentle squeeze. He grinned over at her. She had a way of settling him.

Church was the one place outside his house where people saw Brody without a hat on. When he wasn't wearing the standard issue uniform triple brim campaign hat, he sported a baseball cap. At present his ball cap sat on the bench seat beside him. As much as Jordyn liked the way Brody looked in a hat, she also liked being able to admire his full head of thick, wavy hair.

"Oh thank heavens," he mumbled irreverently under his breath when the reverend finally stopped preaching and asked everyone to stand for the closing prayer and hymnal. The final song had an upbeat tempo and Brody swung his hips, performing a playful jig.

A laugh escaped Jordyn's lips. "Behave," she whispered, pretending to be appalled.

As they descended the steps after the service, Brody walked behind his fiancée, admiring the way she filled out her cream, cable-knit sweater dress and the way her hips swayed in her tall, black boots. He smiled to himself as he imagined her playfully chastising him if he admitted his errant thoughts.

Despite the nip in the air and the snow-covered grounds, the sun was bright and the congregation gathered in the front courtyard to shake hands and engage in so-called harmless gossip. Jordyn gracefully made the rounds, easily engaging in casual conversation. Her pink, flowing scarf billowed around her as she moved seamlessly from person to person. Her scarf matched the natural blush in her cheeks, brought on by the nip in the air.

Brody stood back and studied her flawless approach. While his position as sheriff required a great deal of conversing and politics, it didn't come as naturally to him. He thought of himself as more of an introvert pretending to be an extrovert, preferring a quiet evening at home with Jordyn over crowds and parties.

Kane Masters strode through the crowd with his wife, Molly, on his arm and their two young children in tow. Polished and poised is how an outsider might describe the handsome, young couple. But Brody knew better. Hazards of the job. He knew more about most of the townspeople than he would like. Perhaps that's what made establishing close relationships with them that much harder. He was well liked. That he knew. But other than his fiancée, his mother, two brothers, and a handful of close friends, he never let anyone get too close to him.

Jordyn was unusually quiet on the drive home. She'd felt a spurt of jealousy at seeing Kane and Molly together. And a surge of emotion at seeing Kane in general.

"Any good gossip to report?" Brody teased, breaking the silence.

Offering him her most innocent expression, she asked, "What do you mean?"

"Oh c'mon, don't hold out on me. I saw you talking to Ms. Betty and Mrs. Downey. We both know those two have their ear to the ground and always know the latest on everybody. So, spill it."

She smiled and raised a conspiratorial eyebrow. "Well, apparently, the Shultz's are getting a divorce."

That fact didn't surprise Brody. He'd fielded more than one phone call from concerned neighbors who'd heard shouting coming from the Shultz's residence. But he feigned shock for Jordyn's benefit.

"And Mrs. Downey said that old frame store is closing down. I hate seeing a business fail."

"That's a shame," he said, trying to convey more disappointment than he felt. The frame store was a bit of an eyesore. The owners had moved out of town years ago and had left it to be managed by their son. Their lazy son, who spent more time at the local bars than he did managing the store, and it showed. Brody quietly considered how he'd like to see someone buy the rundown building, fix it up, and make it into a nice place. A place that sold something more useful than picture frames.

"Oh, and Bailey Todd's eldest son was suspended again," Jordyn continued. "Apparently, they found drugs in his locker," she whispered in disbelief.

That tidbit of news did pique his interest. "Did they not call in the authorities?" he asked, sitting up straighter in his seat and tightening his grip on the steering wheel.

"Uh oh. Remember, I'm telling you this as my fiancée, *not* as the town sheriff." It stung a little to use that word aloud, knowing after they'd moved in together, they only got engaged for appearances sake. Brody had made it clear from the beginning he never planned to marry again. The death of his first wife had been too painful. He told Jordyn he didn't need a marriage certificate to prove his love or devotion. And for many years, their arrangement had suited her. But lately...

"Hey, I can take off my sheriff's badge and hat for a couple minutes." Brody grinned over at her.

Rolling her eyes, Jordyn said, "Somehow I doubt that."

"Well, at the very least, as my confidential informant, I promise to keep your identity a secret," he teased.

When she hesitated, Brody prodded. "C'mon Jordyn. I have no interest in getting the Todd boy into trouble. But sometimes you can catch a big fish by applying pressure to a smaller one."

She shot him an impish grin. "And I'm sure Bailey would be pleased as punch about you comparing her son to a fish." But she gave in and proceeded to tell all she knew while Brody took mental notes. Offering drugs to adult tourists was one thing but peddling them to a bunch of impressionable high school kids was an entirely different matter. A matter he couldn't let go without consequences. Not as long as he was sheriff.

Chapter Four

Jordyn's eyes danced around her shop, still in awe that it was hers. For just shy of six years she'd worked tirelessly to transform her love for interior design from a small business run out of her home, to a successful boutique located in the heart of main street. From the quaint, brick storefront of *Homespun Goodness* she sold home décor, custom furniture, and offered her consulting services as an interior designer. To add to the appeal and coax customers through the front doors, she also served fresh baked goods and piping hot coffee. Plain drip coffee with the option of cream and sugar. None of the fancy, highfalutin stuff. Folks knew if they wanted specialty coffee, they could visit *Mugshot Coffeehouse* two doors down.

A bell rang, announcing a new customer had entered. From her perch behind the counter, Jordyn studied the middle-aged woman as she walked in. She was pretty. Perhaps a bit hardened by life. But her beauty was still visible beneath the layers of worry, fine wrinkles, and pancake makeup.

"Can I help you find something?" Jordyn asked.

The woman looked startled, then embarrassed. "No, just browsing, thank you."

Based on the way she kept glancing in her direction, Jordyn knew the lady was doing more than just browsing. Shoplifting was what first came to her mind, hazards of being a shop owner, but she didn't want to assume. The woman looked familiar, but she couldn't place her. Pulling one of her sketchbooks from a drawer behind the counter, as inconspicuously as she could, she began to sketch the woman.

Drawing always helped her to place someone. She drew an oval face with hair piled high. She shaded in the hair to convey the woman's dark, almost raven-colored mane. As she was sketching out the woman's pointed chin, it occurred to her where she'd seen her. She could often be seen on the street corner on the outskirts of town. Panhandling. The locals called her Winnie, though Jordyn doubted that was her real name. Rumor around town was Winnie was doing a bit more than panhandling, but again, Jordyn wanted to give her the benefit of the doubt. She figured a woman had to reach a certain level of desperation to sell herself for money. A level of desperation she had thankfully never reached, and therefore could never understand, so she reminded herself she had no right to judge.

"Would you like a scone?" Jordyn called out after returning the sketchpad to its hiding place beneath the counter. Before the woman could turn her down, she said, "They're on the house."

This prompted a timid smile from the woman, softening the lines on her face that had been etched by troubles and time. Hesitantly she came towards her. From the gaunt expression on her face, Jordyn suspected it had been a while since she'd had a proper meal. Despite her tattered clothing, she was clean. Smelled nice too. Like soap and jasmine. Jordyn supposed the woman would have to maintain a certain amount of cleanliness in her line of work. Her eyebrows were razor thin. It appeared she'd plucked them all out only to draw them back on in two dark, fine lines. Strangely, it made her green eyes pop.

Cheerily, she handed the woman the largest of the scones and said, "My name's Jordyn."

"Gwyneth," the woman replied, nearly swallowing the scone whole. "Thank you. That was delicious."

Jordyn grabbed a Coke from the mini fridge under the counter, popped the top, and handed it to the woman she now knew as Gwyneth. "Also on the house. Helps wash down the scone."

"I'm not asking for any charity." Her tone was defensive.

"Wasn't offering any." Jordyn squared her shoulders, looked the woman straight in the eye, and smiled. "Only friendship and good customer service."

Gwyneth used her tattered shirtsleeve to wipe crumbs from her shiny, red lips. "Well, then, again, thank you."

"You here looking for work?"

Startled, the woman responded, "Um, no."

"Pity. I could use some seasonal help."

She eyed her suspiciously. "What kind of help?"

"Oh, just a few hours here and there at the store. Help me open. Close up. The shop gets pretty busy during the holidays and the place looks like a tornado hit it once the day is over. There's a lot of re-sorting. Dusting the merchandise. Inventorying."

"I didn't see a 'Help Wanted' sign on the door." Her thin eyebrow raised into a point. "You sure this isn't charity?"

"Not at all. Just haven't had a chance to put the sign up yet," Jordyn lied. She figured a lie in the service of helping someone couldn't be all that bad.

The woman frowned, considering. "I don't have a resume or anything."

"You have any customer service experience?"

Gwyneth nearly choked on her Coke, then hid her amused smile behind the red, shiny can. She knew what the townspeople were saying about her.

This time it was Jordyn's turn to feel uncomfortable. She supposed she walked right into that one. She felt her cheeks grow hot but she continued. "I'll tell you what. We'll start you out on a trial basis. Tomorrow morning. Say, seven?"

"Alright." The woman's hardened expression softened a little and she offered what could almost pass for a smile. "Thank you." Her eyes glistened with tears of appreciation. "Truly. You won't regret this."

"Hope not," Jordyn muttered under her breath after Gwyneth made her retreat. She recalled the time she'd brought home a stray dog she'd found while walking home from grade school. She had been enamored with the mangy mutt and thought she was doing the right thing. Right up to the point where the little mongrel bit her. Earned her four stitches on her right hand, a rabies shot, and a long, drawn-out speech from her father about the dangers of bringing home strays. She was now certain there were a few metaphors in his speech but none that she had picked up on at the time.

When Brody called her at the store later to say he was going to be a little late to dinner, Jordyn suggested he meet her in town instead.

"What's in town?"

"Oh, I don't know. Food. Shops. People."

He was silent. Jordyn smiled to herself. Apparently, she was the only one who found her sarcasm funny that day.

"I was thinking we could grab a bite to eat, then go pick out a tree," she explained.

"We already have a tree," he reminded her.

She rolled her eyes. "Thank you, Captain Obvious. I meant a tree for the store."

"Really?" He chuckled. "Now you have to buy and decorate a tree for your store?"

"My store is literally for home décor. I'm not sure how I expect to push the Christmas décor merchandise when I haven't even decorated for Christmas myself."

"Hey, I helped you hang that wreath out front," he reminded her, pretending to be offended.

"Wind blew that off about a week ago."

"Okay, you've twisted my arm. Tree lot it is. Where should we eat?"

"I'm craving Chinese food, actually."

Brody groaned. It wasn't his favorite but he knew how much Jordyn liked it.

From the other end of the call, she smiled to herself. "Kidding," she finally said. "The diner of course. We can get burgers and drinks."

"Now you're speaking my language. See you at six-thirty?"

"Well, maybe you'll be there at six-thirty. I'm starving. I'll be there at six." She hung up before he had a chance to respond.

Brody had thought Jordyn was teasing about the time, but when he walked through the front doors of the diner at 6:25 that evening, he was surprised to see her already sitting at a booth with a half-eaten burger and only a handful of fries remaining on her plate. The waitress was refilling her soda.

Jordyn watched him with lustful eyes as he strolled to the booth and casually took a seat across from her. He had changed out of his uniform and into dark jeans and a white t-shirt. He looked like he'd just walked out of a Levi's commercial. By the shameless stares of the waitresses and female patrons alike, Jordyn realized she wasn't the only one enjoying the view.

"You weren't kidding about six," Brody mused, sliding casually into the booth and seemingly unaware of the beautiful spectacle he made each time he walked into a room.

"I never kid about hunger," she said, grinning.

"Should have realized that." He smiled back at her in adoration before plucking the menu from the table. After perusing its laminated pages for a few moments, he set it back down. He wasn't sure why he bothered to read it over. He always ordered the same thing. The classic burger with an egg on top—over-medium—a side of sweet potato fries. And a Coke.

But even if he had decided to change it up for once, he still wouldn't need to read the menu. He had it memorized. The diner had been serving the same food for as long as he could remember. It was one of the reasons he liked the place. He'd seen the town of Sugarcreek change a great deal over the years. And the changes weren't always for the better. He took comfort in the steadfastness of the diner.

The waitress walked by and asked, "The usual?"

"Hmm…" He stroked his chin as if deep in thought.

Her eyes widened in surprise. She took the pad and pen from her apron pocket and prepared to jot down his order.

"Kidding," Brody told her with a smile. "Usual it is."

Blushing as she smiled back at him, the waitress tucked her notepad back into her apron pocket, stuck the pen behind her ear, then scurried off to put in his order.

Jordyn grinned in his direction. "I still think she has a little crush on you."

"What can I say, people are drawn to the badge and uniform," he said with a wink.

"No, it's just you." Jordyn knew Brody was one of the most liked, most sought-after men in town. It pained her he didn't believe in getting married again. She knew he was devoted to her. But there were moments she feared it could all slip away. Besides the house they shared, she and

Brody didn't have any ties. No marriage certificate. No baby. If he had a change of heart one day, that would be the end of it.

Seeing the troubled expression on Jordyn's pretty face, Brody reached across the booth and squeezed her hand. "Hey, you know I'm never changing my mind, right? There will only ever be you." He was surprised she seemed to need the reassurance.

She smiled, but the smile didn't reach her eyes. She felt a pang of guilt as she realized it was her mind that was no longer made up. She thought of Kane. She also thought of the life she could have had if she'd stayed in New York. A thousand jumbled thoughts went through her brain. She wanted to be open with Brody. She'd always been able to before. But now, she wasn't sure she could. Or that she should. Still, there was so much to say.

"Are you mentally prepared to brave the Christmas tree lot?" she asked instead.

"Looking forward to it," he said with a grin. And they both laughed, knowing it was a boldfaced lie.

Chapter Five

When Jordyn pulled into Marvin's Garage, a lean man came out of the back office, his industrial gray coveralls and boots covered in oil. He carried a clipboard in his grease-stained hands. A pencil and small torque wrench peeked out above the breast pocket of his coveralls.

"Hello, Marv," Jordyn called out cheerily as she climbed out of her car. She'd always had a fondness for the middle-aged mechanic and his doting grandfather vibe.

He smiled back at her, setting his clipboard on the hood of a nearby car and graciously accepting the home-baked blueberry scone she offered him. "Good morning, Jordyn. What can I do for ya?"

"Check engine light came on a few days ago and now the engine's making a funny sound," she said. "Had trouble starting her today too. I'm hoping it's something simple, like a bad distributor cap." She tried to keep a straight face, but the gleam in her eyes gave her away. She knew next to nothing about cars.

Marvin's face split into a wide, knowing grin. "I see someone's been hitting up Google."

She laughed and held up her right hand. "Guilty."

"Let's pop the hood and we'll take a quick look, shall we?"

She reached into the car and pulled the hood release latch, proud that she at least knew how to do that much. Marv walked to the front of the car and propped open the hood. He leaned in, fiddled with some cables and wires beneath the hood, grunted to himself, then stood up straight.

Looking over at Jordyn, he said, "We'll do some diagnostics and then get started on her. Might take us a bit. Do you have things to do?"

"I have a few errands I could run," she said. "But I might need the loaner."

Marvin kept two spare cars at his shop. One was a mid-90's black Honda Civic with rusting, oxidized paint and bald tires. An incredible hunk of junk but it did the job as a designated loaner vehicle for his customers. It was reliable enough for small distances and his customers were always happy to return it. The other car was a 1968 Chevy Camaro—fully restored in Grotto Blue. His pride and joy. He knew Jordyn meant the latter when she'd mentioned she needed a loaner. He'd loaned it to her once in a moment of weakness and she'd fallen in love with the beast.

"Slim's here," he offered, referring to the Honda.

Jordyn shook her head, then pushed her lips into a pout. "C'mon Marv, you know I'll be gentle with her."

"You gonna Google how to drive her properly in the snow?"

She batted her eyelashes, still smiling.

He sighed, giving in. "Fine." He walked to the wall of the garage and pulled the keys off the hook. He hesitated, then handed them over. "Treat her like the lady she is," he said, only half-joking.

"I'll treat her like she was my own," Jordyn said.

He snorted. "That's what I'm afraid of."

With strict instructions from Marvin to make herself scarce for at least three hours while he finished her car, Jordyn had a bite to eat at the local diner, then picked up some groceries. She knew she could head back to the store and help out, but she was giving Gwyneth some space to get acclimated. She was also giving her a chance to work one-on-one with Hailie, who had been less than thrilled by Jordyn's impulse hire but was slowly coming around to the idea of extra help.

On a whim, Jordyn stopped in at the police station to say hello to Brody, but he was out on a call. Disappointed and out of ideas, she checked her watch. She'd barely been gone for two and a half hours, but rather than drive around aimlessly, she headed back to the garage.

When she pulled up, there were two men talking to Marvin. She thought it looked like the men were in an argument. Figuring it was nothing more than a dispute over a repair bill, she pulled into a parking space and started to get out of the car. It was at that moment one of the men punched Marvin square in the gut. He doubled over in pain. Without thinking, Jordyn scrambled out of the car and rushed to help.

"Get back to the car, Jordyn," Marvin screamed out. He sounded winded and his eyes flashed with panic.

The two strangers turned towards her. Jordyn thought one man appeared to be holding a gun in his right hand. She raced back to the loaner car, locking the doors. She reached for her cell to call the police, but the two men strolled back to their car and drove away. Once she was sure they were gone, she scrambled back out of the car to check on Marvin.

"Are you okay?" she asked, running towards him and placing a hand on his shoulder.

"Oh yes, no worries at all. That was nothing." But he winced and held his side.

"Marv, that didn't look like nothing. That man punched you."

He waived it off. "Just a man-to-man dispute about the parts I put in his car."

"But one of those men had a gun."

Marvin gave her a puzzled look. "You're mistaken, Jordyn. Those were just two businessmen from out of town."

Jordyn searched his face. "No, I am almost certain I saw a gun."

"You probably saw his phone. He had a copy of his bill on an email and he was waiving it around at me."

Jordyn couldn't be sure, but she was fairly certain Marvin was lying to her. She knew what she'd seen. Didn't she?

"Hey, hey," Marvin said, putting an arm around her shoulder and leading her towards her car. "You had a bit of a shock, that's all. Sometimes people get riled up about their cars. And money. But there's nothing to worry about. The man still paid and I suspect he's back on the interstate now, headed for home. Your car is ready though."

Feeling foolish, Jordyn allowed him to steer her towards her car.

"It was indeed the distributor cap," Marvin told her.

She perked up a bit. "Really?"

"Nope, kidding," he said with a grin. "Don't shoot though." He put his hands in the air in jest.

She laughed, feeling even more foolish. She supposed she'd let her imagination get the best of her.

"How much do I owe you?" she asked after Marvin helped her transfer the groceries from the loaner to her car.

"It's on the house."

"No, Marv. I can't let you do that."

"I insist," he said. "Least I can do after you've had a scare. Now you take your car and treat it well. And maybe let's just keep today's little incident between you and me, huh? I wouldn't want any of the locals to be scared about visiting my garage. Bad for business," he said with a toothy grin.

Jordyn wanted to tell him she had every intention of telling the sheriff about the incident, but after seeing the pleading look in his eyes, she smiled and said, "It'll be our little secret."

Visible relief washed over Marvin's face. She waved goodbye to him as she drove away, feeling a wave of guilt that she'd just lied to a man she thought so highly of.

Jordyn and Brody sat down to a meal of spaghetti and French bread that they'd both helped prepare. It was the first time in days Brody had been home in time to help make dinner. A fact that bothered Jordyn but she held it in.

"I dropped by the store today," he said.

Jordyn arched an eyebrow in surprise. "Oh? I didn't see you." She had decided not to tell him about the incident at the garage, not wanting to worry him, but now she wondered if she'd have to.

"That's because you weren't there. Hailie said you stepped out for a bit."

"Yes, I did," she said with a smile, not offering anything further.

Brody grinned, enjoying the intrigue. "Well, I know you weren't out Christmas shopping. You've probably had that done since July."

She nodded in agreement but still didn't respond.

"So I've been racking my brain all day about what you were up to."

Jordyn leaned forward, conspiratorially. "And? What did you come up with?"

"Well, I saw the groceries in the fridge. But still, that's not something you'd typically do during the workday."

"You're correct. Do I sense a question in that statement, sheriff?" Her eyes sparkled with amusement. His inquiries didn't bother her. She knew they weren't coming from a place of distrust. Her whereabouts was simply a puzzle he needed to solve.

"C'mon, give me a hint," he begged with his big, puppy dog eyes.

Jordyn pushed back from the table and smiled in his direction. "Okay, okay, since it means so much to you." She shook her head as she refilled her water glass, using the elegant glass pitcher she'd recently purchased at *Christmas for All Seasons*, one of her favorite stores. "You know how the car's been acting funny lately?"

"I didn't realize that, actually."

Jordyn frowned. She'd mentioned it a couple of times but Brody had been so preoccupied lately. She let it go. "Well, it has, so I decided to take it in today to give my new employee time to work without feeling like I was looking over her shoulder. I hired her on a trial basis but I think I make her nervous. She seems to find Hailie less imposing."

He let out a knowing grunt.

"Oh, stop," she said, pretending to be offended.

"I didn't realize you'd hired someone new. She must have been in the back when I stopped by. What brought that on?"

"Well, the store has gotten so busy, but just between you and me, I may have had a soft moment."

"Oh, really? Who is she?"

Jordyn bit her lower lip. "Her name is Gwyneth."

"Gwyneth, Gwyneth..." Brody repeated. His brow furrowed as he tried without success to place the name.

Raising an eyebrow and lowering her voice, she said, "Some people call her Winnie."

"You hired a prostitute!" The astonishment in his tone was almost comical.

"Brody, I'm shocked at you. I hired a woman down on her luck."

He flashed her a guilty grin. "I'm sorry, that was insensitive of me. But Jordyn, are you sure you can trust her in the store?"

"She doesn't work the till. And she's never in the store alone. But I'm a firm believer in second chances."

"You have a heart of gold," Brody told her. "Perhaps a head of mush though," he teased, shooting her a wink before shoveling in another bite of food.

Jordyn studied his mood, still trying to decide if she should tell him about the incident at the garage. He was always so protective. And the last thing she wanted was to make more trouble for Marv.

As if reading her thoughts, he asked, "So, what was the outcome with the car, anyways?"

Holding nothing back, she relayed everything. Even her belief that one of the men had been holding a gun. When she was through, Brody's knuckles were white where he had a death grip on his fork.

"You should have told me this earlier," he said between clenched teeth as he fought to remain calm.

"I know, but I didn't want you to worry. Or to get Marv in any kind of trouble." She stared pointedly at him. "And I may have been mistaken about the gun..." She trailed off.

Brody stood from the table, crossed to where she sat, and pulled her up and into his arms. His hand found the base of her neck. He stroked her cheek with his thumb as he leaned closer and brushed his lips across hers. "You know you can tell me anything," he murmured softly.

But he was wrong, Jordyn thought to herself. There were things she couldn't tell him, and that's what hurt the most.

As they worked together to tidy up the kitchen, she asked cheerily, "What should we do tonight?"

Brody stopped scrubbing the plate in his hand. He set it down and turned to face her, a look of apology in his eyes. "Oh, babe, I'm sorry. I forgot. I'm needed at townhall tonight."

Her good mood instantly fizzled. "Seriously?"

Brody had been taking several meetings downtown but he'd been vague about what they were about. Jordyn was never into politics, so she hadn't pried. But now his frequent late nights were cutting into their time together. And if there was ever a time she needed him to be there for her, it was now.

"I can cancel," he said hesitantly.

"No, it's fine. You should go." Her throat felt thick with emotion. She hated feeling so needy.

His brow furrowed in apology. "I'll make it up to you."

She dried her hands on her jeans, returned the dish towel to the drying rack, and started to leave the room. "I'll just add it to your tab," she said over her shoulder. She headed to her room to take a hot bath. She needed a relaxing distraction.

When Brody called up to her later that he was leaving, she didn't respond. Just as she didn't respond when he returned home that evening and curled up next to her in bed. Instead, she pretended to be sound asleep.

"Love you," Brody murmured in her ear. He was grateful. Grateful to have Jordyn in his life. And grateful she may have unknowingly blown his drug trafficking case wide open. His one regret was that he wouldn't be able to tell her. It was the one thing he hated about his job—that he couldn't share everything with her no matter how badly he wanted to.

Chapter Six

The light in the master bathroom roused Jordyn from a deep sleep. When she cracked her eyes open, she saw Brody already up, pants and belt on, and slipping into his uniform shirt.

"What time is it?" she asked, barely coherent but still not missing the ripple of Brody's muscles as he slid his arms through his shirtsleeves.

"Five a.m. Sorry, babe, I was trying not to wake you."

"Five a.m.!" Sitting up in bed, she rubbed the sleep from her eyes. It wasn't unusual for Brody to wake up early, but it was unusual for him to be off to work so soon. He typically grabbed a quick workout from home. After his shower, they'd usually enjoy a cup of coffee together on the sofa before they both headed into work.

"You have to go in this early?"

He sighed. She could hear the regret in his voice. "I promised Beatrice Harper that I would help her with some things around her place before I went into work."

"I see." She frowned, crossing her arms in front of her chest.

Brody studied her expression. Usually such a caring person, Jordyn never used to complain when he was called away to run errands that went beyond his job description. But lately she seemed more withdrawn and he suspected him frequently being called away was adding to the strain.

"Jordyn?" he spoke softly.

She shrugged but didn't answer him. Instead, she stared down at her hands, twisting her diamond engagement ring around her finger. Her eyes narrowed in contempt at the slender platinum band with the round, brilliant cut stone, despising what it represented. A perfect fit—yet a shining promise of a marriage that would never be.

"Jordyn?" His voice sounded tortured.

Still no answer. It wasn't that she was ignoring him, exactly. She simply couldn't find the words to convey what she was feeling. Mrs. Harper was recently widowed, and probably genuinely needed someone to lean on, but it didn't mean Jordyn had to like it. At least Beatrice had the fortune of once having a husband and sharing his name, she thought bitterly. Her chest tightened and she pulled the covers to her chin.

"I just wonder when you'll make the time to help me for a change," she said, breaking the silence. Her tone was more resentful than she'd intended.

Even as she said the words, she knew there wasn't anything she needed help with. She also knew she was picking a fight. It's what she did when she was feeling insecure and unhappy.

Brody was about to ask what she needed help with, when she interjected with, "After all, I stayed in this crummy little town for you. The least you can do is try to be there for me instead of being so concerned about every other citizen."

Bitter tears stung her eyes but they didn't carry the same sting that her hurtful words did for Brody. He loved Sugarcreek. And up until that moment, he'd thought she loved it too.

He took a sharp intake of breath. "Jordyn, I don't know where this is coming from, but if this is about having a baby, you're not the only person who's hurting here." Despite his own pain, his tone was tender.

She softened, but still wasn't ready to let him off the hook. Or ask for his forgiveness.

When she didn't answer, Brody continued. "Babe, if you need me here, I can stay."

"Why do I have to *need* you to make you stay?" she said bitterly. When they'd first met, she'd been drawn to his selfless nature and overwhelming need to help others. But lately she felt like he was there for everyone else but her.

He sat down on the edge of the bed. "Jordyn, I know you haven't been happy lately. I only wish you knew how badly I could change that for you." He stroked her cheek and tucked a strand of her chestnut hair behind her ear. "I know you sacrifice a lot to be with me. But you know my job."

She nodded, ashamed by her overreaction. She looked up into his soft, brown eyes and saw the agony behind them. "I do know," she said. "I'm sorry, Brody. I'm just not myself lately."

He leaned in and kissed her. Softly at first, then with more urgency. She closed her eyes and allowed herself to pretend everything was okay between them.

Once his sensuous mouth released hers, he asked, "How about a date night tonight?"

Her eyes lit up and the anguish she felt subsided. "Really?"

"Yes. Just you and me. Decent restaurant. We can even get dessert." He placed a hand on her cheek and stroked her soft skin with his thumb.

She grinned. "Well, you know I can't resist dessert." Then she asked playfully, "You sure you don't want to ask if Mrs. Harper wants to join us? Cozy table for three?"

Brody shook his head, then pulled her in for a lengthy kiss before heading out.

Taking advantage of having the house to herself, Jordyn gave it a quick scrub, then got busy wrapping Christmas presents. Always the planner, she'd had most of the presents purchased and stashed away for months. The real trick was hiding Brody's gifts in places he wouldn't think to look. Since he was a police officer, she suspected he knew exactly where she hid them and was too polite to admit it. But each year, upon unwrapping her presents to him, he feigned surprise perfectly.

Jordyn meticulously wrapped the carefully selected gifts, tied the packages with pretty bows, and placed them under the Christmas tree. She stepped back to admire the tree Hailie had helped her decorate days earlier—but only after she'd given Jordyn a lecture about the faux pas of decorating for Christmas before it was even Thanksgiving.

Each ornament that hung from the tree had a special meaning. Many were gifts. Others, hand-crafted ornaments Jordyn had picked out over the years. But the ones most dear to her heart were the ones she'd had since childhood. Her mother had left them to her and she cherished them all. Admittedly, the less attractive ones were hidden towards the back. As an interior decorator sometimes sentimentality had to take a backseat to the element of design.

It was still too early for the shop to open, but Jordyn figured she'd go in and get an early start. Perhaps take inventory and rearrange some of the merchandise. She used the drive in to unravel her feelings. Nobody knew the pain she carried. Some days it snuck up on her out of the blue. But most days it rode shotgun beside her, a constant gnawing.

The person who she wished she could confide in most was the one person she knew she couldn't tell. Marriage was off the table from the beginning. Brody had made it clear. She'd accepted it. At the time. If she admitted to him that her feelings had changed, she didn't know what that would mean for them. Throw in two years of not being able to have a baby with him and she felt like a failure. And like their relationship was on shaky grounds despite how happy they'd always been.

When she reached the store, she was startled to find a seedy character mulling around on the street corner. His shifty eyes gave Jordyn the sense he was up to no good. The man was reed thin and appeared to be at least a foot taller than her. His stringy hair hung down in his face, masking most of his features.

She quickly unlocked the door and slipped inside, immediately locking it behind her. Deadbolt in place, she felt temporarily secure. Until the man came up to the door and started knocking on it.

"We're closed," she called out as calmly and friendly as she could. Despite her efforts, she could hear the waiver of fear in her voice.

"I've got something I think you'd be interested in," the man said.

His tone was menacing and Jordyn shrunk away from the door. She closed the blinds and pushed a chair under the door handle. "I'm calling the police," she yelled out.

The man continued to rattle the doorknob. Despite the potential danger, Jordyn kept her wits about her. She had lived in New York City by herself after all. She could handle an unruly character. She called Brody's cell. No answer. More annoyed than frightened at that point, knowing Brody was likely helping Mrs. Harper and hadn't heard her call, she dialed 911 instead. She recognized the calm, pleasant voice as Meghan Downey's, the dispatcher commonly on duty.

"Meghan, it's Jordyn Reilly."

"Brody's not in yet, Ms. Reilly." The dispatcher sounded friendly but confused why Jordyn would call the emergency number.

"Yes, I understand. I need a squad car sent over to my store right away. Someone is trying to break in."

"Right away, ma'am. Hang on the phone while I dispatch a unit to your location."

While she waited, Jordyn pushed a smaller display case in front of the door and chair as she continued to talk to Meghan. The display case wasn't heavy enough to fully barricade the door but she reasoned it would provide a small barrier of protection between her and the stranger if he managed to kick in the door. Both ladies were doing their best to keep the other calm. Meghan asked how the store was fairing. Jordyn inquired about whether Meghan had begun her Christmas shopping. Despite the eminent danger, the awkwardness of the small talk was evident. After a few moments, Jordyn no longer heard the man outside her shop door, but she wasn't taking any chances. She asked Meghan about her plans for Christmas day.

After several minutes of silence from outside, a loud knocking on her shop door made her heart jump into her throat. She shrieked unexpectedly at which point Meghan piped up that a squad car had arrived.

"It's Deputy Carter, Jordyn," the officer called out, confirming what Meghan had already said. "If you're there, please open up."

She'd met Deputy Billy Carter a few times. He had a tall, gangly build. Almost frail. Long, spindly fingers. Stooped shoulders that gave away his insecurities over his towering height. Not to mention he was five years her junior. Just a kid. A rookie on the force. Not her preferred knight in shining armor to save her from an unscrupulous character, but under the circumstances she figured she couldn't be picky. She thanked Meghan and hung up the phone.

"Just a second," she called out to him. She slid the display case away from the door and removed the chair she'd wedged under the handle before unlocking the door and opening it to the officer.

"Hi, Billy," she said, visibly relieved by his presence and out of breath from her unexpected furniture rearranging.

"You okay in there?"

She sighed. "Yes. Someone was trying to get in but he seems to have lost interest." She stepped aside to let him in.

Billy nodded, then stepped into the store and closed the door behind him. "I canvassed the street a bit before I came to the door. I didn't see anyone."

"Well, trust me, there..."

"Hey, I believe you," he reassured her, resting a slim hand on her shoulder. "I'm sure Brody's told you all about how we've had an increase in crime these days. Mostly petty stuff. But we've had some drug trafficking."

Jordyn smiled tightly but didn't respond to his comment. She couldn't. Because if she did, she'd have to admit that Brody hadn't mentioned any of these things to her. And to add insult to injury, the moment she'd truly needed him, she'd gotten his undernourished, rookie deputy instead.

By the time Hailie arrived at the store, Deputy Carter had taken Jordyn's statement, recanvassed the area, and was long gone. Jordyn had been too rattled by the morning's events to do the inventory she'd planned, so she perched behind the counter and tried to make sense of everything she was feeling. When she heard the jingling of Hailie's keys in the door, she realized she'd forgotten to unlock the store and turn the sign from Closed to Open. Hailie wasn't scheduled to start work until thirty minutes past opening time.

"Sorry, I must be undercaffeinated," Jordyn explained at seeing the questioning look on her friend's face when she walked through the door of the shop. Hailie closed the door behind her and switched the sign to Open. Upon doing so, two customers who had been patiently milling around outside came walking in.

They weren't locals, so Hailie used her most professional tone and said, "Feel free to look around, and please don't hesitate to ask if you need any assistance." Then she beelined for the counter so she could get the scoop from her dear friend about what precisely had been going on with her lately.

Jordyn had barely finished conveying her story to Hailie (in hushed tones as not to scare off the customers) when Brody came barreling through the front door of the shop. Clearly, he didn't see the need to worry about what the customers might think, because he came in looking like he was about to shoot up the place if anyone stood in his way of reaching the counter Jordyn stood behind. Not waiting for permission, he circled around the counter and wrapped her in his arms.

"I was worried about you," he said, breathing a sigh of relief into her chestnut hair.

"Not enough to answer your cellphone," she pointed out.

"Baby, I am so sorry. I left it in the truck while I was helping Mrs. Harper."

Rather than console her, his excuse pained her, so she didn't respond.

"If anything had happened to you…" His voice trailed off. "I wasn't aware you were going to the store so early." He cradled her face in his hands.

She pulled away from him. "I guess you're not the only person in this relationship who doesn't clue the other person in on key information." She knew she was being obnoxious, but the hurt she felt, coupled with fresh memories from her terrifying experience, were getting in the way of her keeping a level head.

"What's that supposed to mean?" he asked with a blank stare. His tone wasn't angry. He seemed legitimately confused.

She let out an exasperated sigh. "Deputy Carter told me…" She paused, looked around, then continued in a more hushed tone. "He told me that there's been an increase in crime in the area," she hissed. "Would have been nice to know." She crossed her arms in front of her chest. Mostly to hide the fact that her hands were still trembling from her brush with danger. The adrenaline was still coursing through her body.

"I'm so sorry, Jordyn. I didn't want to worry you." He realized he was using the same excuse she had for not immediately telling him about the incident at Marvin's Garage. He made a mental note to start filling her in more—although there were still things about an active investigation that he wasn't at liberty to disclose.

"So, me being ignorant and unprepared is a better option?"

He drew out a breath slowly. "No." When he reached up to stroke her hair, she pulled away from him.

"Jordyn, I really am sorry. Usually when you get to the store it's daylight out and the streets have more people. I miscalculated the danger." He tipped her chin upwards, forcing her to meet his gaze. "I promise it won't happen again."

By now the morning rush had started and customers were filing in one after the other. Jordyn took another step back. Her look softened, but only because she wanted to put a temporary end to an argument she wasn't prepared to have in front of her customers.

"It's okay," she said, even though they both knew it wasn't. "We can discuss this later."

Brody frowned and a deep crease appeared between his eyes. It was the same crease he always got when he was worried about something. He opened his mouth as if he intended to say more. Instead, he planted a soft kiss on her forehead. "I'll see you tonight. I can come help you lock up if you'd like."

"No need," she said, offering her frostiest smile. Then she turned to help a customer without sparing him another glance.

Chapter Seven

The successful sting operation to bust the drug trafficking ring was the highlight of Brody's month and gave him immense satisfaction. The raid was a joint task force between his men, the FBI, and the DEA. Since local law enforcement was instrumental in the break in the case, and it had been Brody who'd alerted both the FBI and DEA in the first place, both agencies were amenable to working with the local authorities rather than taking over. Brody's men proudly stood shoulder to shoulder with the FBI agents during the raid while the DEA ran point from a command center.

Months of investigations and stakeouts led to enough evidence for Brody to feel comfortable bringing in the outside agencies. Local law enforcement wasn't equipped with the manpower or the tools to bust such a large operation. But it was the incident Jordyn experienced at Marvin's Garage that turned Brody's focus to Marv and the possibility that his garage was a front for the organized drug ring. He'd been right, and he had Jordyn to thank, even though he hadn't been able to tell her. Not until an arrest had been made.

Although Marvin and his crew were the ones arrested, it was clear someone else was calling the shots. Marvin was just a pawn. But despite how hard local law enforcement and the DEA leaned on him, the garage owner wouldn't give anyone up. Brody left the station frustrated, and hopeful he'd be able to keep the arrest out of the papers until he had time to explain it to Jordyn.

He planned to fill her in that evening, but when he came home, she met him at the door, devastated by yet another negative pregnancy test. She was late, she'd informed him days earlier. They'd both been hopeful. But once again those hopes were cruelly extinguished. He'd spent the evening consoling her, forgetting all about the exciting break in the case that had led to Marvin's arrest.

The incident at the store was only the beginning of Jordyn's unraveling. When she read the morning paper announcing the drug bust at Marvin's Garage, she felt like Brody had betrayed her. She was starting to resent him for reasons that weren't entirely his fault.

Still, she was both bitter and disappointed that he hadn't told her about Marvin. How did the media get to know things before she did? After stewing on the matter while ducking Brody's phone calls all day, she picked a fight over dinner.

"Maybe if you were around more often, we'd have a minute to be intimate and, I don't know, actually conceive a baby."

The resentful words she flung at him were like tiny barbs that hooked into his heart and slowly bled him dry. It wasn't like her. Jordyn was usually so kind.

Brody knew she was hurting. He took a deep breath and let it out slowly. "Maybe there's someone you should talk to about how you've been feeling," he stated calmly.

"I'm talking to you," she snapped. When he didn't react, she let out a heavy sigh. The man had the patience of a saint but she was pushing him to the breaking point.

"You're right," she said after a pause.

"We can go together."

"No, I'm the one with the problem, I'll go myself," she said, more harshly than she'd intended. But the hurt look in his eyes had her backtracking. "I mean, unless you wanted to go with me?"

Brody stared at his beautiful fiancée, searching for the best way to respond. He knew she needed him. But he also knew she hated admitting any weakness. He searched for the words to convey his support without making her feel like he was swooping in to save her. She didn't play damsel in distress very well.

Finally, he said, "We're a team. I'll play any position you need me to."

Her expression softened, and she asked with a smirk, "Any position?"

His face split into a wide grin. "You have a one-track mind," he teased. "But yes."

Brody had worked with Dr. Barbara Keller on a few cases in the past. She was one of the best therapists around, and not just because she was one of the only therapists in his one-horse town. Dr. Keller was well respected amongst her peers and often consulted with other therapists and psychiatrists amongst the larger cities in Colorado. Brody set up the appointment himself. He had a feeling Jordyn would try and talk herself out of it if he relied on her to make the arrangements.

"Sure, I can squeeze in a few sessions," the doctor told him over the phone. "Is this a friend of yours?"

The pause on the other end of the line told her everything she needed to know. "I see," she said. "So, couples therapy, then?"

He hadn't thought of it that way until that moment. He just thought Jordyn needed someone to talk to. In a more professional capacity. But perhaps they did need somebody to talk to as a couple. If not being able to have a baby was causing them this much distress, something else might be broken. And as the advice he'd heard for years echoed in his head—you can't expect a baby to fix a relationship—he found himself saying, "Yes, couples therapy."

"Couples therapy isn't admitting defeat," Dr. Keller reassured him. "It's the first step in admitting you're ready to fight for something you believe in." Despite her words, the doctor was surprised Brody and Jordyn were seeking therapy. From what she'd witnessed, they were that adorable sort of couple who didn't have to show an overwhelming public display of affection, yet everybody could tell they were madly in love. It was the stolen glances. Or the casual way he'd touch her shoulder or elbow as he passed her in a crowded room.

"Thanks Barbara," Brody said, dropping the formalities in appreciation for her friendly vote of confidence.

"I can make an opening for you tomorrow if that works. How does seven a.m. sound?" It was earlier than she typically opened her practice, but she didn't let on.

"I'll have to check with Jordyn, but that would be greatly appreciated. If you can fit us in, we'll make that work."

"I'm happy to squeeze you in," she said.

Jordyn's and Brody's relationship was one everybody envied. Folks with kind hearts rooted for them to succeed. Others, more prone to jealousy, secretly hoped for the demise of their seemingly perfect relationship so the happy couple could wallow in misery with the rest of the planet. Barbara was the former—she was wholeheartedly rooting for them.

Even though Brody had the appointment all set up, Jordyn still tried to make excuses not to go. It was after Brody told her he planned to go with or without her that she changed her tune. He didn't miss the worried look in her eyes when he mentioned he'd booked it as a couples therapy session. He hoped it conveyed the magnitude of the situation.

Despite Jordyn dragging her feet, she and Brody arrived early to the appointment. Dr. Keller's office was pleasant. The furnishings were similar to what one might expect. A caramel-colored leather chair for the doctor.

An overstuffed tan sofa lined with brightly colored throw pillows and a rectangular coffee table positioned in front of it. The coffee table held outdated magazines and a fine layer of dust. The overhead lighting was soft and subtle. Not the harsh, fluorescent lights Jordyn imagined.

The couple sat next to each other on the sofa across from Dr. Keller who was already perched in her chair, notepad and pen in hand. Brody slung an arm around Jordyn's shoulders and she leaned into him.

The doctor smiled. "Well, that's a good sign," she said. "For some couples I see, it takes months of sessions to get them to this level of intimacy."

Brody grinned. Jordyn blushed.

"First of all," Dr. Keller said, "I want to set the stage for these sessions. This is a safe environment. Both of you need to feel free to say whatever you're feeling, even if you think it might upset the other person. And likewise, your partner will have a chance to respond to those feelings."

When the couple nodded, indicating they understood, she continued. "Now, I will intervene if it's starting to feel more hostile than productive. And speaking openly shouldn't be misconstrued as a chance to sling mud at each other. But I think you get my point."

"We're not the sort of couple who slings mud at each other," Jordyn said. Even she noted the defensive tone she'd failed to mask.

"Well, as I said earlier, another good sign. Now, let's start with talking about why you *are* here. Jordyn, if you'd like to go first."

Jordyn frowned. She wasn't sure she was ready to discuss her problems with a complete stranger. But beyond that, she wasn't sure how they'd gotten to the point where couples therapy was even necessary. She stole a glance at Brody, pleading for intervention.

He cleared his throat. "I can go first. That is, if it's okay with you, Dr. Keller?"

"Sure, go ahead." She gestured in his direction, then returned to scribbling in her notepad.

"Well, I'll just cut right to the chase. Jordyn and I have been trying to have a baby."

"I see." That much she had already heard. It was a small town, after all. People talked. And the handsome, unmarried sheriff was often a hot topic of conversation. "Go on," she prodded gently.

"Well," Brody said, stealing a glance at Jordyn before continuing. "It seems like we're having difficulty conceiving. And lately..."

Dr. Keller leaned forward in her chair. It wasn't until Jordyn squeezed his hand that Brody felt comfortable continuing. "Well, lately it's caused a strain on our relationship."

"Uh huh. What sort of a strain?"

"Pardon?" he asked, shifting in his seat.

"Increased fighting? Anger? Perhaps a financial strain if you've been trying alternative methods?"

He pressed his thumb into Jordyn's palm. He didn't want to mention it was his fiancée who seemed to be cracking under the strain. He also didn't want to sound like he was blaming her for their problems and not taking any responsibility of his own. But when she still didn't pipe up, he continued.

"Well, with the stress of my job, I probably take that home sometimes, so maybe that makes it harder for Jordyn to tell me how she's feeling..."

This time Jordyn did interrupt. "Brody's just being kind. The problem is mine alone. I'm angry that I can't have a baby. And if we're being honest here, I probably take it out on Brody because he's around." Her cheeks colored at the shame of admitting aloud what she'd been unwilling to even admit to herself.

Brody frowned. He disliked seeing the woman he loved taking all the blame. "We deal in different ways," he said. "I've been burying myself more in the job. This town."

Jordyn snorted.

"I think we've touched on something there," Dr. Keller said. "Jordyn, what Brody just said seemed to hit a nerve. Let's discuss that more."

"Nothing to discuss," she said with a shrug. "Brody's always loved this town. He's always put his heart and soul into it…"

"And that bothers you." It wasn't a question. The therapist was making a declaration.

Jordyn didn't show a hint of emotion as she said, "What kind of person would I be if it did?"

Brody squeezed her hand. Dr. Keller smiled and said, "A woman who loves her husband…"

"Fiancée," Jordyn cut in, correcting her. The bitterness in her tone wasn't lost on anyone in the room. Brody shifted uncomfortably in his seat.

"Pardon, a woman who loves her *fiancée* and maybe hasn't been able to lean on him as much as she'd like. Maybe you think he's abandoned you at a time when you need him most. That he's giving priority to others over you."

Brody's eyes whipped to Dr. Keller's.

"Just conjecture," the doctor said, putting up her hands to demonstrate she meant no offense.

His frown deepened, but he wasn't angry. He'd been so focused on his work as a coping mechanism, he hadn't realized it was making Jordyn feel abandoned.

"Jordyn, I'm so sorry," he said, turning to face her.

"Stop. I won't let you take the blame for this. I suppose I could take the easy way out and claim my anger is because I feel abandoned. But it goes deeper than that."

"Then tell me," he prodded.

"There are things I need to sort out on my own." Then directing her attention to the therapist, she said, "I think I'd like to do solo sessions in the future."

Brody gently skimmed his thumb over the top of her hand as he masked his hurt. Moments ago he'd thought they were making progress. Felt they were working towards something together. Now he felt like Jordyn was keeping secrets she wasn't willing to share. And again, he feared whatever was going on with them went deeper than not being able to have a baby.

"If that's what you want," he said.

"It's what I need."

Chapter Eight

Dr. Keller prepared herself for the morning session with Jordyn. Even as a seasoned therapist, she had to admit she was a bit nervous. Brody and Jordyn had always seemed to be on such solid ground. She feared Jordyn might reveal she had fallen out of love with Brody. And since she greatly admired the sheriff, she hated the thought of seeing him go through a heartbreak.

Jordyn took a seat on the sofa and crossed her long legs, trying to appear composed.

"Can I get you a bottled water or some tea?" Dr. Keller offered.

"I'm good, thanks."

"Okay, then let's get started. First of all, I want to make it clear that anything you say here will be kept confidential. Even if you and Brody choose to come back for another couples therapy session, nothing you reveal to me will go beyond the two of us. Understood?"

Jordyn nodded.

"Perfect. Now let's start with why you're here today."

"Because I'm a fraud!" she blurted out.

Dr. Keller concealed her reaction. "Let's explore that more. What do you mean by that?"

The tears started to flow as Jordyn told the therapist all about her anger for being trapped in a small town. How she felt she'd tricked Brody into a relationship—never revealing her dreams to live in a big city. And finally she admitted she now wanted an actual marriage. Something she was certain Brody would never agree to.

After sitting in silence for a few moments, absorbing everything Jordyn had revealed, Dr. Keller said, "Now, tell me...you've been with Brody for how long?"

"Six years."

"Okay, six years. And during that time, when would you say this longing to move back to New York began. Right away?"

Jordyn thought about it. She remembered how crazy she'd been about Brody from the start. Geography hadn't seemed like much of a factor at the time. "Definitely not right away. I'd say maybe a year or so ago."

"I see." The doctor jotted something down in her notepad. "And when did you and Brody start trying to have a baby?"

Jordyn blushed. "It's been two years." She wasn't sure why she felt so ashamed to admit it. The cold, hard truth made her feel like such a failure. As a partner. As a woman.

Dr. Keller's pen scribbled across the pages of her notepad. It reminded Jordyn of how engrossed she herself got with her sketches while she was designing a room.

"I see." More scribbling. "And at what point did you start worrying you might not be able to have a child?"

"About a year ago," Jordyn admitted sheepishly.

"Okay. So, around the same time you started becoming dissatisfied with Sugarcreek."

"I never said I was dissatisfied with it."

Dr. Keller raised an eyebrow.

Jordyn sunk back into the couch and crossed her arms in front of her chest. "Well, okay, but I never used those exact words."

"Let's continue," she said patiently. "Do you believe a big city would be a better place to raise a baby?"

"Well, it doesn't seem like I can *have* a baby, now does it?"

The doctor pursed her lips and clicked the top of her retractable ballpoint pen.

"Sorry, I'm just on edge."

"That's okay. This is a safe space, remember? So let's say Brody is interested in moving. Or he gives in."

"I wouldn't ask him to do that."

Noting her patient's defensive tone, Dr. Keller replied, "Okay, but relationships are about compromise. So humor me. Let's pretend you move. Big, bustling city. The restaurants. The parties. Lots of culture."

Jordyn nodded and her eyes lit up. "Exactly, you get it."

"Yes, I do. I was single in a big city once. Okay, so now fast forward a few months and you find out you are pregnant. Would the city still be as appealing?"

"People raise babies in the city all the time."

"They do," she agreed but her tone was noncommittal.

"Well, it's not like we wouldn't ever go out just because we had a baby."

"Of course. Date nights are still important after children." She set down her notebook and tucked her pen behind her ear. "I want you to do something for me. I want you to close your eyes."

"This isn't the part where you hypnotize me, is it?"

Dr. Keller laughed. "No, I'm afraid I don't possess that talent. This is really more of a visualization exercise. Close your eyes."

Jordyn obeyed.

"Okay, now I want you to picture a time when you and Brody were most happy. Can you do that? It doesn't have to be a particular place, but it's more about focusing on a feeling. I want you to concentrate on how you felt during that time. Okay?"

"Okay," Jordyn whispered. Her eyes were squeezed shut.

"Do you have that feeling?"

"Yes." Thankfully, the feeling wasn't as far away as she imagined it might be.

"Okay. Now, I want you to hold onto that feeling, but now picture yourself with a newborn baby."

Jordyn's eyes snapped open, revealing the pain behind them. "Seems cruel," she said flatly.

"Trust me, Jordyn. Please. Just close your eyes and imagine it."

She closed her eyes and drew out a long breath. It took her a few moments to find the feeling again she was so desperate to hold onto. It took even more concentration to picture herself with the baby she wanted more than anything in the world. She had to push past the hurt. The countless disappointments when another month came and went without a confirmed pregnancy.

"Let me know when you can picture it."

"I'm trying," Jordyn whispered in earnest.

Dr. Keller's voice was warm and soothing. "Take your time. Just concentrate and picture yourself rocking the baby to sleep. Picture Brody there with you."

Eyes still closed. Jordyn's frown transformed into a smile. "I can picture it," she whispered. A peace settled over her countenance and her tone was one of wonderment.

"Okay. Where are you at?"

"We're in our living room."

"Describe the scene for me."

The doctor's office melted away and the new image Jordyn saw played out like a movie in her head. She visualized every detail. She furrowed her brow in concentration, taking it all in. "Brody and I are sitting next to each other on the sofa. The baby is nestled in my arms. It's a girl, wrapped in a pink, fluffy blanket. She has beautiful, sandy blonde hair like Brody's. Brody's holding her bottle. The T.V. is playing softly in the background. The fireplace is casting a warm glow. The curtains are drawn, blocking out the rest of the world."

Dr. Keller remained silent for a few moments, letting Jordyn soak up the scene in her head. Then she asked, "And what's beyond those curtains?"

"The outdoors. I don't know. Grass. Trees." Jordyn said with confusion.

"Where, Jordyn?"

"Sugarcreek," she responded, as if stating the obvious.

"Okay, you can open your eyes."

When Jordyn opened them, Dr. Keller was smiling.

"So, not the city?" the doctor asked.

Jordyn didn't respond but her mood clouded.

Unfazed by her patient's sullen expression, she continued. "There's nothing wrong with dreaming of something more. But sometimes when there's something we want so badly, but it's out of our control, we start replacing that desire with something we think we *can* control. Does that make sense?"

Jordyn knew Dr. Keller was referring to her longing for the big city, but the image of Kane popped into her head instead. "I see," she said, only partially convinced.

The sophisticated watch the therapist wore around her sturdy wrist made a faint beeping sound, indicating the session was coming to a close. "I'm afraid that's all we have time for today. But I'd like to meet with you again if you're up for it. I think we've made some real progress here today."

"Sure," Jordyn said, noncommittal. She wondered what sort of progress they'd made, really.

"Just make an appointment with reception on your way out."

As Jordyn turned to go, Dr. Keller said, "Just one more thing."

Turning back around, she asked, "Yes?"

"You're not a fraud, Jordyn."

Jordyn responded with a wan smile but she wasn't entirely convinced. After all, the therapist couldn't read her thoughts. And if she could, she'd probably see that Kane occupied them with more frequency than Jordyn was willing to admit.

When she returned home, she found Brody outside chopping wood. They had plenty of wood to last them the winter. Probably two winters. But it was something he did when he was working something out in his head. Or if he needed to be alone.

"I'm back," she called from a safe distance behind him.

He turned, nodded in her direction, then raised the axe again. He brought it down hard on the chunk of wood, splintering the log in two. When it became abundantly clear he wasn't in the mood to speak to her, Jordyn shrugged her shoulders and wandered inside. She figured he must still be smarting from being disinvited from the therapy sessions he'd worked so hard to arrange. She couldn't blame him. She'd be angry too.

Chapter Nine

Brody's stomach knotted when he woke up to find Jordyn wasn't lying next to him. They'd gone to bed angry, but he'd assumed they'd talk it out in the morning. Panicking, he scrambled out of bed and jerked on his clothes. He grabbed his keys from the nightstand, prepared to drive to *Homespun Goodness* and hash things out. But his panic turned to surprise when he entered the hallway and found the house aglow with Christmas lights and scented candles. He wandered to the kitchen, following the sound of Christmas music playing softly from Jordyn's phone.

"Smells good in here," he said, treading lightly.

Jordyn spun around from the stove. "Blueberry scones," she said with a smile. She wore a festive apron over her flannel pajamas.

Brody was happy to see she appeared to be in a good mood despite how they'd left things the night before. But he still proceeded with caution. He'd given her the silent treatment. Something he'd typically never do. But he'd wanted her to know how it felt. She'd been unusually quiet towards him lately. Almost broody.

He knew the incident in the store had rattled her, and perhaps was to blame for her recent mood swings, but there seemed to be more to it than that. And more to it than her disappointment of not having a baby if she'd just be honest with him. She'd been distant. As if she was purposely shutting him out.

Brody crossed the room and kissed her lips, longing to repair whatever was wrong between them. Jordyn kissed him back. But when he reached for a scone on the cooling rack, she swatted his hand. "Hey, they're for the church bake sale." He didn't miss that her typically playful demeanor had a bit of a bite to it.

Truth being told, she'd made plenty of extras, but she still hadn't fully forgiven him for not being there for her at the store, or for Marvin for that matter, and was inclined to deny him the baked goods in a passive-aggressive attempt to punish him.

He'd apologized many times of course. And it was obvious how guilty he felt. But for Jordyn it didn't change the fact that she'd felt abandoned and left in the dark, as irrational as her feelings might be. She'd been prepared to stay mad at him until he somehow made it up to her. But at seeing his crestfallen face and knowing how much she'd hurt him the day before by choosing to go to therapy alone, she softened. "I do need a taste tester."

Recognizing the peace offering, he grinned and moved in closer to her. "Well, I'll probably need to sample two or three to offer an informed opinion. You know, to ensure consistency."

"If you feel you're up to the challenge," she teased, temporarily forgetting her efforts to be mad at him. "I'll save you three of them. One for here, and two for the road."

Once Brody left for work, Jordyn's mood soured once more. She tried to control her sullen thoughts as she finished cleaning up the kitchen and waited for Hailie to arrive. She'd chosen to close the store that day so she could prepare for the church bake sale, and Hailie was coming over to help transport the goodies to the big event.

By the time Hailie arrived, Jordyn had finished baking, had cleaned the kitchen, and was sitting in the living room next to a crackling fire. She placed a plate of freshly baked goods on the coffee table, knowing her dear friend would need some bribery before they got to work. Hailie walked through the front door without knocking and plopped down on the couch beside her.

Ordinarily Jordyn only needed Hailie to show up for her mood to be lifted. But today her mere presence wasn't doing the trick. "Thanks for coming," Jordyn told her once she realized she was brooding.

"You know you don't have to twist my arm." She grinned, then popped a piece of a scone into her mouth. "Although, full disclosure," she said between bites, "I'm here for the food."

"Well, hopefully it makes up for the lousy company," Jordyn said with a frown.

Patting her hand, Hailie said, "You're not lousy company."

Jordyn narrowed her eyes.

"Well, I mean you're not the *worst* company. At least you offer sustenance."

Once Hailie polished off her last bite of dessert, the two friends headed to the kitchen to start boxing up the baked goods.

"Is there any flour left in the great state of Colorado?" Hailie teased as she helped Jordyn load the baked goods onto trays and then into boxes for transport to the church bake sale.

"Hey, it's for charity."

"Still, it's an awful lot of food. You sure you're not baking to fill a void?"

At seeing the pained look on her friend's face, Hailie instantly regretted her words. "I'm sorry, Jordyn. Very insensitive of me. That came out wrong."

"No worries." she said, managing a laugh. "Truth hurts sometimes."

"You know, you're luckier than most. You have a dreamy fiancée who adores you. This great house." She looked around, then grinned as she looked back at Jordyn. "The best friend anyone could ask for."

Jordyn laughed and gave her friend a sideways hug. "I know," she admitted. "Hailie, what is wrong with me? It's like I know how good I have it. I'm with a man who dotes on me every chance he gets. I'm my own boss—running a store that allows me to pursue my passions. But still, somehow, it's not enough. I want more."

She took a seat at the kitchen counter and bit into a cookie shaped like a Christmas tree. "I want a baby more than anything. But on top of that, I also miss New York. I miss Broadway plays and hotdog vendors. I miss crowds and car horns."

"Have you ever thought of planning a vacation there?" Hailie followed her friend's lead, taking a seat and reaching for a snowman shaped cookie that was almost too cute to eat. Almost.

She shook her head. "Nah. Brody hates big cities. He moved here to get away from that life. I couldn't ask him to go back to it."

"But he can ask you to give up your dreams?"

"He doesn't know," Jordyn admitted quietly.

"What?" Hailie was stunned. She assumed Jordyn and Brody talked about everything.

Jordyn drew in a breath, then exhaled slowly, considering her next words. She hoped she wasn't betraying Brody by what she was about to reveal. He never talked to anyone but her about his past. Very few locals knew about his reasons for coming to Sugarcreek.

"Do you know he used to be a cop in San Francisco?" she finally asked.

"I'd heard rumor. Rumblings here and there that he was some *big city* cop."

"And did you also know he was called to a crime scene that involved the murder of his wife?"

Hailie blinked in surprise. "I hadn't heard that part. Wait, Brody was married before he came here?" She was blown away, and a little hurt that

Jordyn had never told her, although she thought she understood why. Her best friend was faithful to a fault. And once something was revealed to her in confidence, it remained a closely guarded secret.

Jordyn nodded, then continued. "When we first met, he told me about his late wife. He told me about why he left San Francisco, looking for a quieter lifestyle. I knew all of that when I started dating him. I also knew he never wanted to get married again. Losing his wife had been too painful. I knew that's what I was signing up for when I agreed to be in a committed relationship."

"So?" She blinked in confusion.

"So, I went into this relationship under false pretenses. I agreed to live the small-town life. Agreed I didn't need to get married. I pretended to be someone that maybe I wasn't when I ensnared Brody into being with me."

"You *hardly* ensnared him," Hailie reasoned. "I've never seen anybody look at someone the way Brody looks at you."

Jordyn shook her head. "I doubt he'd look at me the same if I told him I long to go back to New York. To finish school and get my degree in interior design. I long for culture, champagne, and parties."

Hailie knew it wasn't champagne and parties her best friend longed for. Quite the opposite. Sure, she had loved New York. And yes, she was clinging to her dream of working in a big city as a highly sought-after interior designer. But Hailie knew what Jordyn really wanted was to get married and have a baby. And the longer she felt she couldn't have those things, the more she looked for something to fill the void and searched for things to blame for the emptiness she felt.

She knew some day her friend would need to face all these things. Eventually, she would need to come to terms with her emotions, if not for her own sake, but for the sake of her relationship with Brody. She also knew at some point she might need to mention this and to help Jordyn process her feelings no matter how painful it might be. Perhaps the therapy would help.

"How did your first solo therapy session go?" she finally worked up the nerve to ask.

"We talked about New York. Can you believe she actually suggested my obsession with moving back there really stems from wanting to be in control?" Jordyn fumed, relieved that Hailie brought it up. She hadn't realized how much she needed to discuss her therapy session with someone. Brody hadn't asked for any details and she hadn't offered him any.

"The nerve," Hailie said. She smiled impishly. This doctor was good.

"You agree with her?"

"Well, I mean, it makes some sense…"

"What, are you two in cahoots?" Jordyn teased.

"Look, I'm not saying you don't miss the city. But I mean, you and Brody could take a trip. The store's doing well. You can leave it in good hands. I know you have the savings for it. But if you're really interested in having a baby, a sudden move to a big city doesn't seem to make sense."

"Why is everyone so convinced I can't raise a baby in the city?" She wasn't as defensive with her friend as she'd been with her therapist.

Hailie laughed. "Nobody is saying that. I'm just saying that once people have a baby, usually the conversation is about safer schools. Smaller towns. This seems like the opposite. Which is what makes it seem…I don't know. Misplaced somehow."

"Well, heck, you could have mentioned all of this earlier and saved me a hefty therapy bill," Jordyn said with a grin.

"Oh no, I still plan to send you a bill," Hailie said, shooting her a wink. "And once you get it, you may go running back to your therapist."

"Doubtful." She thought about her next appointment and wondered if she should cancel.

"Can I offer you some free advice though?" Hailie asked after a few moments of silence passed between them.

"Nothing's stopped you before," Jordyn said with a laugh.

Hailie chewed on her bottom lip as she struggled for the correct words. Then she said, "I know you like adventure. But be careful not to confuse comfort and stability with being bored. You really are lucky to have someone to come home to that you feel...safe with."

Reaching across the counter, Jordyn gave Hailie's hand a squeeze. She felt a surge of guilt for being dissatisfied with what she had with Brody. Knowing the relationship hell that her best friend had gone through before she'd come to Sugarcreek.

"Anyway, enough about that," Hailie said, gently slipping her hand out of Jordyn's and smiling brightly. "I'll tell you what. It might not be New York, and this might not be a party. But we do have champagne." She held up the seven-dollar bottle she'd brought with her, then poured both herself and Jordyn a glass, adding a splash of cranberry juice to hers. She drained the glass, savoring the flavors on her tongue.

Jordyn smiled. Hailie was so full of life, despite her past hardships. It reminded her of herself not so long ago. "You know, you're the only person who doesn't make me feel bad about drinking before noon."

Eyes twinkling, Hailie laughed. "I am a terrible influence."

"Yes, yes you are." Raising her glass in salute, she said, "And I wouldn't have it any other way."

"Is Brody going to make it to the bake sale?" Hailie asked, breaking the silence on their drive to the grange hall where the church bake sale was being held.

"He said he's gonna try." She didn't try to mask her sullen expression.

Hailie offered a sympathetic smile. "I'm sure he'll be there."

"Yeah, if he's not caught up saving a cat from a tree or helping some elderly woman across the road." She said it with more biting sarcasm than she'd intended. After a pause, she grinned and said, "Wow, I am a terrible person. Look at me being angry with a man for being the perfect gentleman and town hero."

Laughing, Hailie said, "Well, your secret's safe with me."

"What about Tom?" Jordyn asked, switching the subject and trying to channel a more positive attitude. "Will we be seeing him today?" She raised an eyebrow.

The question made Hailie blush. Tom Lacey owned the local hardware store. Jordyn had introduced them, and although he and Hailie were both too shy to admit it, they were mad for each other.

"I guess we'll see," she said. Her eyes brightened and her tone was hopeful.

Gwyneth smoothed down the sweater dress she'd borrowed from Jordyn as she waited just inside the front entrance of the grange hall. She'd offered to help set up for the bake sale and Jordyn had gladly accepted her help—even offering to pay Gwyneth for her time, which she had politely refused.

Upon seeing her, Jordyn gave her a big hug. Hailie offered an awkward wave and smile, then wandered off to find the booth assigned for Jordyn's baked goods.

"That dress looks far better on you than it does on me," Jordyn said with a genuine smile. "I'm going to have to insist you keep it." She seemed oblivious to the gawking stares and didn't appear at all embarrassed to be seen with someone most locals speculated was a prostitute.

Gwyneth, however, was fully aware that all eyes were on her. She knew what the townspeople thought of her. Most of the rumors weren't true, but she didn't feel the need to dispel them. But despite the cruel gossip, Jordyn had shown her nothing but kindness and compassion. Gwyneth wanted to offer her something in return. Mind made up, she smiled quietly to herself. She had just the thing.

When Tom Lacey entered the grange hall, he glanced around in anticipation. He wasn't big on crowds and his typical nature would be to position himself close to an exit. But this time he made a beeline for Hailie. Jordyn took it all in from where she stood behind her booth. She was impressed by Tom's boldness. She'd always liked him. His large nose was the first thing you noticed about him when he walked into a room. But the next thing you noticed was his kind eyes and warm smile. Those agreeable aspects served to balance out his features. Folks who took the time to work through his barrier of shyness and get to know him saw him for the uncommonly wonderful man he was.

"Good evening, Ms. Reilly," a smooth, familiar voice interrupted Jordyn's nosiness. She jumped, realizing she'd been caught staring at Tom as he made his move. Her focus shifted and she felt an unexpected fluttering in her stomach at seeing Kane Masters approach her booth.

Rich, powerful, good-looking. She could all but see herself peeking over the fence and admiring the greener pastures on the other side. Standing over six foot-three, his cowboy hat added an extra couple of inches to his soaring height. He wore a plaid, pearl button up shirt that he tucked into his tight Wranglers. His alligator skin boots were a bit flashy for Jordyn's taste, but if anyone could pull it off, it was Kane.

"Good evening, Mr. Masters," she said, trying to compose herself as she straightened the trays of cookies. She looked up into his gray-blue eyes, then looked away, rearranging cookies on their trays for no useful reason.

He cocked his head to the side and grinned, revealing his large dimples. "Oh, c'mon Jordie. You know you can call me Kane."

Her stomach did flipflops at hearing the old nickname he had given her in high school. She'd hated it at the time. Now, she felt drawn to it with burning nostalgia.

"Kane," she said. She liked the way it felt when she said his name. It felt intimate. This time she met his gaze, enjoying the way his stormy gray eyes burned into hers.

He smiled, quietly studying her.

"Congratulations on the baby," she blurted out, unable to bear the silence that passed between them.

"Thank you." He grinned proudly. "My brood seems to be growing."

The familiar pang of jealousy returned. "You hoping for a girl or a boy?" she asked. He and Molly might want it to be a surprise, but she figured Kane still had to have a preference.

"Just healthy."

She admired the way his smile brought out his dimples and the faint laugh lines around his eyes.

"What about you?" he asked. "You plan to give up your big-city dreams and settle down with a family?"

His words pained her. Not only because she couldn't seem to get pregnant, but also because Kane knew her in ways that Brody never would. Never could.

"I never did apologize for how abruptly I ended things so many years ago," she said, full of regret.

"Nah, forget about it," he said with a nonchalant wave of his hand. "I only remember the good stuff."

"We did have some pretty good times in high school, didn't we?" she asked, grasping at old memories. Surely her question was innocent enough, she told herself.

"We sure did," Kane said with a boyish grin. Then his eyes twinkled with mischief. "I miss those times sometimes."

"How much for the scones?" a man's voice broke in, interrupting the moment.

"Two dollars apiece or twenty for a dozen," Jordyn said.

The man bought two dozen scones, twelve lemon and twelve cranberry-orange, then wandered to the next booth, leaving Jordyn and Kane alone again.

"What would you like today, Mr. Masters?" she asked, their intimate moment spoiled.

"Did I say something wrong, Jordie?"

"You know I always hated it when you called me Jordie." She placed her hands on her hips, pretending to be cross with him.

He smirked, unoffended. With her pursed lips, he knew she was trying to convey her disapproval. What she didn't realize was the expression brought out the dimples in her cheeks, making her look even more adorable.

"I'll take three dozen cookies," he said, his eyes dancing with amusement.

"What kind?"

"Assorted. I like variety." His gaze held hers.

She didn't miss his innuendo. Or his seductive grin. "Three dozen it is," she said brightly.

"How are the sales going?" Brody's voice interrupted their playful banter.

"You made it," Jordyn said, straightening her spine as she felt her cheeks warm. "It's going well. Everything's selling like hotcakes."

Brody placed his hat on the table and stared into the flushed cheeks of his beautiful fiancée. As sheriff, he had a keen power of observation.

But more than that, he knew Jordyn inside out. He could see what was going on before his eyes. He also knew she and Kane had history. Up until that moment, he'd thought that's exactly what it was. Ancient history.

"Heard congratulations are in order," he told Kane, raising an eyebrow.

"You hear correctly. I figure there's no greater victory than giving my woman exactly what she wants." He tucked his thumbs into his beltloops and rocked back on his heels.

The sheriff's eyes narrowed. "Is that so? Tell me, when I responded to a call at your house last week, was that what she wanted?"

Kane scowled. "You really should learn to mind your own business." His tone held a warning.

Jordyn slammed her palm on the table, annoyed by the fight unfolding before her as if she weren't standing there. "That's enough," she demanded. She glared coolly at the two handsome men before her.

"Kane, sweetie, are you ready to head home? I'm feeling tired." Molly appeared out of nowhere, her sing-song voice interrupting the confrontation. She placed her perfectly glossed lips into a pout.

Kane slipped an arm around his wife's slender shoulders. "I'm ready, baby-doll."

"Enjoy the goodies," Jordyn said, tempering her jealousy as she handed over the boxes of cookies, each tied with a pretty, green bow.

Kane reached into his pocket and pulled out a hundred-dollar bill. "Keep the change," he said, handing the bill to Jordyn.

Her fingers grazed his as she took the crisp bill. She felt the familiar sparks of electricity. Sparks that had laid dormant since graduation day when she'd announced to him that it was over. That she was pooling every nickel she'd scraped together from endless nights and weekends of babysitting and housecleaning, plus a modest academic scholarship, and leaving for New York to pursue a bigger, better life.

Brody joined Jordyn on the other side of the booth and put a protective arm around her waist. "This bake sale is a real success. Proud of you, honey."

He kissed her cheek and she leaned into him, feeling his support and warmth. It used to be all she thought she'd ever need. But in that moment, her heart faltered. She watched as Kane walked away with his pregnant, beautiful wife and found herself longing to trade places with Molly. Kane believed in marriage. He was a family man who seemed set on having lots of children. He also understood Jordyn's love for the big city and had the means to move anywhere. For the first time, a powerful wave of regret swept over her, threatening to swallow her whole. Tears stung her eyes as a ringing began in her ears.

"Jordyn, you okay?" she heard Brody ask. He stepped back to study her.

But her eyes were trained on Kane and the way he confidently strode through the crowded grange hall, stopping to shake hands or say a few words to the other townspeople. The room began to sway and her vision blurred out of focus. Through tear-filled eyes, the image of Molly holding hands with Kane faded and was replaced with an image of herself. She could imagine holding Kane's hand and heading towards the exit, towards the perfect life they would share.

"Jordyn?" Brody said in a concerned tone. He sounded far away. "You look pale. I'll go grab you some water."

She watched him disappear into the crowd. Glanced over once again at Kane and Molly, who'd made it to the middle of the grange hall. The ringing in her ears was replaced by a roaring sound. Like the ocean. Jordyn felt the dizziness set in. She reached for the edge of the table to steady herself, missing it completely. A gasp escaped her lips as she fell, helpless, to the concrete floor that swayed beneath her weary feet.

Chapter Ten

Jordyn awoke feeling more rested than she could recall in recent weeks. The pillows felt fluffier. If she didn't know better, she'd swear they were made of authentic goose down feathers and not the cheap imitation her neck most mornings made her painfully aware she'd skimped on. The mattress felt softer. Plush. She rolled over on her back and pulled the navy-blue sheets over her head to block out the sunlight streaming through the windows. The sheets were silk, she realized. They felt expensive. As the room came into focus, she realized the king-sized bed she was lying in was not her own. She shot up in bed and pulled the covers to her chin.

"Jordie, what's wrong?" The concerned, masculine voice was familiar—but it wasn't Brody's.

She whipped her head around. Lying next to her was Kane Masters looking sexy, bare-chested, and very much not like her fiancée.

"Wha...what happened? What did we do?" She peeked under the covers and gasped at her nakedness beneath. "Did I get drunk at the fundraiser?"

Kane chuckled and his gray-blue eyes danced with humor. "Drunk at a fundraiser? I sure hope not."

There was a soft knock on the door, then it swung open and a little girl wandered in wearing fuzzy pajamas. With one hand she rubbed the sleep from her bright blue eyes while she dragged a teddy bear behind her with the other.

"Morning my sleepy princess," Kane told the little girl. He patted the comforter beside him and the girl skipped over to him and bounded onto the bed.

Jordyn remained confused and concealed beneath the covers.

"Mommy, Mommy, guess what I dreamed last night?"

Jordyn stared at the little girl with the dark ringlets and cherub face who stared expectantly back.

After shooting Jordyn a strange look, Kane looked at the little girl and said, "Mommy might not be quite awake yet." He then turned his focus back to Jordyn. "You going to answer your daughter?" he teased.

The room spun. What was she doing in Kane's bed? And why was he insisting this little girl was her daughter?

"Please excuse me. I'm not feeling well," she responded. She darted out of bed and headed to the bathroom, hoping her naked streaking wouldn't permanently scar the little girl who'd just called her *Mommy*. She didn't need to stop and ask where the bathroom was. She'd been in this room before. Several times in fact. It was the master bedroom in Kane Masters' house. It wasn't decorated the way she'd done for Molly and Kane. Molly had different taste. She wasn't without taste. It was just different. The room now, Jordyn realized, was decorated exactly how she would have done it had she free rein. Neutral color pallet with bold accents stylishly mixed in. An appealing selection of textures to make the room visually stimulating without being overwhelming.

She shut the bathroom door behind her, then rushed to the sink to splash cold water on her face. To her credit, she didn't throw up. But when she looked in the mirror, another wave of shock ran through her. Her hair was dyed a platinum blonde. Blonde! She thought it made her look pale. And a little bit cheap. Upon closer inspection, she noticed a bruise on her forehead, above her right eyebrow. That wasn't terribly unusual given she was a bit of a klutz, but she couldn't recall doing anything to cause the bruise.

She reached up to touch her injury. Felt the lump beneath her skin. But what startled her even more was seeing the reflection of her nails in the mirror. They were long and polished in a deep red. Acrylic nails if she wasn't mistaken. Ordinarily she kept her nails cut short. It was low maintenance and with her endless furniture projects, the short length helped keep the paints and wood stains from getting under her nails.

She let her perfectly manicured fingertips wander to her midsection. She peered down at her stomach, curious how her body had faired with a pregnancy if the little girl in the next room truly was her daughter. Her close examination left her pleasantly surprised. Her abs were more defined than she was used to. Evidence that she must be into working out in whatever bizarre dream she was having. Two tiny stretchmarks on her left buttocks, almost invisible to the naked eye, were the only evidence of a postpartum figure.

"You okay in there, hon?" she heard Kane ask from the other side of the door.

"What's wrong with Mommy?" a tiny voice asked.

"Nothing, Aubrey," she heard Kane assure the little girl. "Mommy's just tired this morning. Why don't you go find Frida and see if she can make you those chocolate chip pancakes you like so much?"

"Okay, Daddy."

Once she heard the bedroom door close, Jordyn opened the bathroom door and walked to the bed. Kane was sitting atop the covers, half-naked, with his back resting against the headboard.

Jordyn plucked a silk robe from the floor, wrapped it around her and pulled the belt tight. After she sat down next to Kane, she asked hesitantly, "Um, what did we do last night?"

"Glad it was so memorable," he said with a smirk. Then his brow furrowed once he realized Jordyn wasn't teasing. "You're starting to worry me," he said. "Maybe that knock to the head you took yesterday did more damage than we thought." He pulled her face close to his and kissed her forehead.

Gingerly, Jordyn touched the bruise on her brow. "What did happen?"

A deep crease lined Kane's brow. "You really don't remember anything?"

Jordyn shook her head, *no*.

He exhaled slowly, cast her a strange look, then began. "You were on the stool in the kitchen, looking for something from one of the top cupboards and somehow the stool toppled over and you hit the edge of the counter on your way down. Knocked you out cold. I had the doctor check in on you but he said you were going to be fine." He cupped her chin in his palm and peered into her eyes. "I'm starting to wonder if he was wrong."

Jordyn touched her forehead once more. "I'm sorry, I'm just so confused. We're married?" She hoped her surprised tone didn't sound like she was repulsed.

"Have been for ten years now." He studied her to see if she was messing with him.

"But that means…"

"That I married my high school sweetheart right after graduation. Sure does." He nodded proudly, then planted a kiss on the tip of her nose.

Jordyn was stunned. She'd never gone away to college. Never studied interior design. She wasn't with Brody.

"My parents…"

"I'm sorry, hon. They died. Six years ago. Car accident."

Jordyn dipped her head and murmured a small prayer for her mother and father. That much hadn't changed. A tragic car accident had claimed the lives of both her parents her senior year in college. She'd taken a temporary leave from her education to come back to Sugarcreek for the funeral. As the only child, it was left up to her to sell her parents' old house and to settle any other financial matters. She felt the familiar bitterness at having her parents taken from her so soon. And guilt that before they'd passed, she'd only taken the time to call home about once a week. At the time she'd been convinced she was too busy to call more often. Funny how one doesn't realize what's important until it's gone.

"Babe, you're really starting to worry me," Kane said in reaction to Jordyn's silence and crestfallen expression. Concern was etched across his handsome face as he reached over to stroke her cheek. Observing her flushed complexion, he felt her forehead to check for a fever.

"I'm fine. I'm fine," she said, more to convince herself than him. "So, we're married. We have a daughter." She spoke slowly, waiting for her own words to sink in.

"Aubrey," Kane said proudly.

"Aubrey," Jordyn said breathlessly. She'd always loved that name. "Who is …" She took a stab in the dark. "Five?"

"Four," Kane corrected.

"Four, of course. And my parents have passed on. And the town sheriff is…" She trailed off, hoping her loaded question wasn't too obvious.

Kane frowned and drew out a long breath. "Sheriff Brody Kingston. The biggest thorn in my side."

She felt relief that in whatever alternate reality she was experiencing, Brody remained sheriff. At least that much was a constant. But what was happening? She had to be dreaming.

"And what day is today?" she asked.

"Wednesday."

"Oh no, what time is it? I'm going to be late for the store." She scrambled out of bed, still a bit disoriented.

"The store? Sweetie, if you have something urgent you need to buy, just send Frida."

She stopped and looked at him. "Frida? Who's Fri… Never mind. No, I mean I need to go into work."

"Work?" Kane's puzzled expression would have been comical if Jordyn wasn't so confused herself.

"Yes. *Homespun Goodness*. My store." She was exasperated at having to explain the obvious. "I can't leave Hailie there by herself again."

"Okay, I'm going to call a doctor. Now you're starting to scare me."

"Why?" By this time Jordyn was near hysterics.

"Sweetie, you don't work at any store. You have your hands full here, what with this house. And Aubrey."

She frowned and sat back down on the bed. Of all the times she'd imagined being married to Kane and living in his big, grand house, she'd never pictured herself staying at home full time. "And what about Hailie?" she asked softly.

"I'm afraid we don't know anyone named Hailie," he said gently. "Hon, I'm so sorry."

A sob escaped Jordyn's lips and she buried her head in Kane's chest. What had become of her beloved store? Of Hailie? Of the life she'd known.

Kane stroked her hair and let her cry. Despite her sorrow, she couldn't help but notice his intoxicating scent or how firm he felt as he held her close. She remembered kissing him all those times in high school. Remembered how good he'd felt each time he'd taken her in his arms. He'd been her first love. Her first in so many things. It had pained her to walk away from him. To leave him behind to pursue her big-city dreams. Perhaps she was being offered a second chance.

Jordyn pulled back from their embrace and stared into his concerned eyes. She recalled the one occasion, as a child, where her parents had taken her to see the ocean. The thrashing waters and misty skies had seemed to fuse together in a stormy, clouded gray. Even as a young girl, she'd been mesmerized by the magnificent beauty before her. Kane's piercing eyes matched that memory.

With a tender hand, he stroked the bruise on her forehead. His fingers trailed to her hair and he gently pulled her towards him. His lips felt warm as they landed softly on the place of her injury.

Despite not understanding what was going on, Jordyn felt a tingling sensation. Arousal, perhaps. She smiled as she allowed the sensation to surge through her. That feeling of something new. And forbidden.

Despite her protests, Kane insisted that she see a doctor. She dressed quickly, not recognizing her clothes. Or her makeup. The woman she'd been wore minimal makeup and bought whatever brand was on sale. This new person she seemed to be had two cases full of makeup and it was obviously expensive. There were lip liners, and lipsticks in every color. She settled for what she was comfortable with—powdered foundation, black mascara, and a subtle application of gloss to her lips. She packed the rest of the makeup away, wondering if the new her actually wore all those shades of lipstick and eyeshadow. She hoped not.

She was about to return to the bedroom when Kane came up behind her. She spun around to face him, heart hammering. Tenderly, he stroked the bruise on her forehead once again. She winced, but her eyes remained focused on his.

"I'll help you cover that up," he offered.

Jordyn was startled. "No, that's okay," she started to say, but Kane was already pulling the makeup cases back out from under the vanity.

With expert precision he applied the concealer, then a light dusting of powder over her bruise. "There, good as new," he said proudly.

"Wow, you're a miracle worker with this stuff," she exclaimed as she studied her reflection in the mirror, still trying to get used to her platinum hair. "I can hardly see it."

He shrugged and put the makeup away. "I'm not without skill," he teased.

After arranging for the housekeeper to take Aubrey to preschool, Kane drove Jordyn to her doctor's appointment. She found it sweet the way he held her hand the whole way there. When they reached the doctor's office, the receptionist handed her a clipboard with forms to complete. Jordyn sat down in the plastic waiting room chair and stared at the top page. Her eyes blurred with tears. Address. Marital status. Last name. These were questions she no longer felt confident she knew the answer to.

Kane touched her softly on the shoulder. "I'll do it," he told her. Gently, he tugged the pen from her fingertips and relieved her of the clipboard with the pages of forms she had no interest in completing.

"We're married," he reminded her, as he checked the appropriate status on the form. His tone was both soft and reassuring as he walked her through the questions he completed on her behalf. "Masters," he spoke aloud as he filled in her full name. "You told me you were proud to share my last name."

Jordyn offered a wan smile in acknowledgement of a past she had no memory of.

He'd just finished the final page when a nurse came into the waiting room and announced, "Mrs. Masters. The doctor will see you now."

It took her a few seconds to remember that she was now Mrs. Masters. It sounded strange to her ears and she half expected Molly to saunter through the front doors of the doctor's office. Instead she found herself being whisked to an exam room in the back. Kane stayed by her side. The nurse measured her height and weight. Jordyn was surprised to discover she was ten pounds lighter than she was used to. Clearly this new version of herself didn't enjoy sweets as much. Jordyn was never heavy. Always considered herself reasonably thin. But now, looking down at her legs and stocking feet, she noticed she now bordered on scrawny. She made a mental note to bake some scones and indulge a little. Life was too short to deprive oneself of desserts.

She changed into the thin hospital gown she was offered, then she and Kane sat in the exam room in silence, waiting for the doctor. They didn't have to wait long. There was a soft knock at the door, then the doctor entered. She was a pretty, middle-aged woman with short, blonde hair and an athletic build. She stood a couple inches taller than Jordyn.

"Where's Dr. Crowst?" Kane asked. He sounded irritable, and Jordyn gave his hand a reassuring squeeze. She figured he must be worried about her.

"It's his day off," the doctor explained. "I'm doctor Gena Landers. I'm the on-call physician today."

"I was expecting Doctor Crowst," Kane repeated with a degree of obstinance.

"I'm sure Dr. Landers will be just fine," Jordyn interrupted, embarrassed by Kane's surly tone. She cast an apologetic look at the doctor.

"I assure you, Mr. Masters. Your wife is in good hands."

Jordyn smiled. "We have no doubts."

"If you could sit on the edge of the table, please."

Dr. Landers did a series of routine tests. She listened to Jordyn's heartbeat and lungs. Shone a flashlight in her eyes to look for signs of a concussion. At least that's what Jordyn assumed she was doing. The doctor asked a series of questions. What year was it? Who was president? Those Jordyn could answer. But then she asked, "When's your anniversary?"

Without thinking, she rattled off the anniversary of her first date with Brody. At seeing Kane's look of horror, followed by the doctor's worried expression, Jordyn's face turned scarlet. "I'm sorry," she apologized. "I'm not sure where that date came from."

The doctor patted her knee reassuringly. "Why don't you start by telling me everything you do remember."

Jordyn took a ragged breath. "I remember my childhood. I remember high school. But after that…" She trailed off, not certain where the gap began. She'd already learned she hadn't gone to college. She hadn't ended up with Brody. Apparently, she'd married right after high school— a fact that horrified her. She'd always felt strongly that nobody should make such an important decision at an age when they barely qualified to vote or purchase cigarettes. She remembered what her father had said when some of her friends chose matrimony over college. *If you're too young to legally buy the champagne for your wedding night, you've got no business getting married.*

"And you remember nothing about being married to Kane? Nothing about your relationship?" The doctor's calm tone penetrated her thoughts.

"Oh, I remember us dating through most of high school," she chimed in, hoping that part of her past remained unchanged so she didn't appear to have completely lost it.

Kane grinned. It seemed to bring him comfort that she at least remembered pieces of their past together.

Jordyn continued. "But I don't remember us getting married." She paused, guilt-ridden. "I don't remember having a child," she said in almost a whisper. The shame at forgetting something that important made her feel like a failure.

The doctor frowned, obviously concerned. "And how did you receive the head injury?"

"I don't recall that either," Jordyn admitted. She recollected falling in the grange hall during the bake sale, but that fact didn't appear to be true in this alternate reality she couldn't seem to wake up from.

"She was standing on a stool getting something out of the top kitchen cupboard. The stool toppled over, and she hit her head on the edge of the counter on the way down."

The doctor's eyes narrowed in concern. She leaned in closer to examine Jordyn's head. Jordyn squinted against the harsh fluorescent lighting in the room coupled by the glare from the flashlight.

"Looks like it was quite a nasty fall," Dr. Landers said. "You're lucky that memory loss and a bruise are your only ailments. A fall like that could kill someone."

Jordyn nodded, lost for how to respond. "Will my memories come back?" she finally asked. What she really wanted to ask was, "Is this life real? And are all my memories since high school just a product of my imagination?" Her heart ached at thinking of Brody. Wherever he was, she hoped he was happy. Then again, she'd met him after college. Maybe he didn't even exist. She dismissed the thought, knowing she was being dramatic and recalling that Kane had already told her that Brody remained sheriff.

The doctor paused, deep in thought. Although she was a small-town doctor, she'd completed her residency in Seattle. In the crowded emergency room, she'd diagnosed more than her fair share of head injuries. But this one was unusual, even in her vast experience.

"I'm going to send you over to Sugarcreek General. We'll get you a CT scan. But otherwise you seem very healthy. Based on pupil dilation, I'm not seeing any signs of a concussion." She felt around on Jordyn's skull. Her latex gloves created static, standing Jordyn's bleached hairs on end.

"No additional bumps or other skull trauma," she continued with her observations. Then she stepped back and removed her gloves slowly. She turned her back to her patient, tossed the gloves in the trash and washed her hands in the sink. The smell of the disinfecting soap filled the room but not as much as the silence.

"Well?" Kane, who had been unusually quiet during the examination, finally blurted out.

The doctor turned around from the sink and smiled at him. Although Jordyn suspected she had used the handwashing routine to buy herself some time, when Dr. Landers turned to face them, she appeared completely composed. And confident. "We'll get the CT scan to see what's going on, but at this time, I have no reason to believe your memories won't come back fully."

Jordyn sighed with relief. Kane stood from his chair, extending his hand to shake the doctor's. "Thank you, Doctor Landers. We appreciate it."

She shook his hand, still smiling. "I'll have the front desk fax the order for the scan over to the hospital right now. If you two want to head that way, they'll be ready for you when you get there."

"Will I be admitted?" Jordyn asked. She hated hospitals and the thought of spending the night in one when she was feeling so vulnerable made her feel queasy.

"No. In fact, I'll make a call. Make sure we can skip the emergency room lines. You'll still check in through that entrance, but they should be able to get you in right away. I'll give you a call tomorrow once I've had a chance to review the scans. We can do a consultation by phone unless there's something more in depth we need to discuss." She patted Jordyn on the shoulder. "You just get dressed. Start acclimating as much as you can to your surroundings. I suspect those memories will be back in no time."

"Well, that's a relief," Jordyn said once the doctor had left the room.

Kane handed over her clothes. She felt strange getting dressed in front of him but she didn't let on. She could see him eyeing her. Lust and curiosity settled over his gaze.

"I'll tell you what," he told her. "After your CT scan, we'll go home, get you into a hot bath. I'll have Frida cook you up a nice, warm meal. Then you and I can sit in the living room, look through pictures and talk about old times."

Jordyn smiled up at him. Dang, he was handsome. And seemed so loving to her. If there was an alternate reality to be stuck in, she thought to herself, this would be the best outcome. Once she was dressed, she stepped towards him and placed her hands on his chest.

"I don't deserve you," she said. Then she stood on her tiptoes to reach his lips.

He bent down and kissed her. She could feel his need as he pressed against her. The image of Brody popped into her head, but quickly vanished. This was her second chance, she told herself. Her chance to have everything she ever wanted. She smiled as her lips roved over Kane's. She remembered how it had been when they'd dated in high school. He had always been passionate. A bit broody at times but she assumed he'd long since outgrown that. But what she now recalled most clearly—he'd been a good kisser.

When his tongue swept inside her mouth she said, "I think a few memories are coming back." The memories were further back than Kane was likely thinking, but she didn't mind the mild lie. It made them both feel better.

"Let's get out of here," she whispered through muffled kisses.

"I can think of something else we can do after that bath," Kane teased.

"Then let's skip the CT scan," she suggested.

The man who was now her husband took a step back and studied her. "Honey, that CT scan isn't going to hurt. It's just a scan."

"I know," she said with a shrug. "But honestly, I feel fine. I'm sure this memory gap is only temporary, and the CT scan isn't going to help get my memory back any faster."

She moved towards him again and slipped her slender arms around his waist. "Being together. Doing the things we love to do together. That will help."

Kane stroked her cheek, then kissed her softly once more. "Okay," he said. "But if your memories haven't improved over the next couple of days, I'm marching you straight into the emergency room and I'll give you the scan myself if I have to." His tone was firm, but his eyes gleamed with mischief.

"Deal," Jordyn laughed. "Now let's go home to Audrey."

"Aubrey," he corrected.

"That was a joke," she said with a grin.

Kane's lips thinned in disapproval, unmoved by her attempt at humor. His face was etched with worry.

Realizing she'd misjudged the situation, Jordyn tried to alleviate his concern. She sidled up closer to him and whispered in his ear. "After that bath, I can think of something that might help get my memories back."

Despite her boldness, her heart hammered in her chest. She inhaled deeply, appreciating Kane's intoxicating scent of aftershave and leather. Her hands trailed down his chest, admiring his firmness as her body hummed with excitement.

His large hands cradled her face and his eyes burned passionately into hers. "We could try to remember right now," he teased, glancing at the lock on the closed exam room door.

Jordyn giggled but backed away. "No way," she laughed. "I may have lost my memory, but I haven't lost my sanity."

"It was worth a shot," he said with a shrug. "Now let's get you home and out of those clothes."

She hit him playfully on the shoulder.

"Hey, I meant, and into a bath."

"Sure you did," she said with a laugh.

They left the exam room and walked towards the front desk, holding hands.

"The hospital's expecting you," the receptionist said as they scurried past her.

"Thank you," Kane called out over his shoulder.

Once they were outside, the couple raced through the parking lot like two teenagers skipping school.

Chapter Eleven

When Jordyn awoke the next morning, still in Masters Manor, and still as Kane's wife, she was surprised, but much of the earlier shock had worn off. When she opened her eyes, Kane was sitting up in bed and staring down at her. He reached across the pillow and smoothed her hair. She stared longingly over at him.

"You know, you look like an angel when you sleep," he told her.

She smiled shyly and snuggled up closer to him.

He twisted a lock of her hair around his finger then gently touched the bruise on her brow. "Your memories coming back to you?"

"Almost," she lied. She wanted their life together to be real. Part of her hoped all the memories Kane and Aubrey seemed to have would all come flooding back. And somehow, her memories with Brody would fade off into the distance along with the guilt she carried for leaving him behind.

"I'm happy to have my wife back." He squeezed her thigh and planted a kiss on her cheek.

"Happy to be back," she said, thrilled to bear the title of *wife* but unsure if she could measure up to the person Kane thought she was. She thought of Molly and her designer clothes and polished look. She glanced down at her own manicured nails, wondering if she had the energy to keep up such a rigorous grooming regimen. But she pushed the self-doubt away and sidled up closer to her husband. "Now let's lie here all day," she cooed.

When she felt Kane stiffen beside her, she realized he must have other plans.

"Oh, are you working today?" She wasn't sure exactly what her husband did. The Kane she knew always had some sort of business deal or another in the works. She reckoned his cattle ranch alone was enough to keep him occupied.

"Unfortunately. And I'll be late tonight." He shot her an apologetic look.

"Bummer." She didn't know if she could stand being in that big house by herself after the staff left and Aubrey had gone to bed. "How late?"

She thought she caught the faintest flicker of annoyance on his handsome face, but as quickly as it appeared, the look was gone and was replaced by a soft look of concern. "Not sure. Pretty late. I'm sorry, I know I've had to work late more often these days." He gave her hair a playful tug.

Jordyn nodded, uncertain how frequent his late nights away had been. Then she smiled to herself, realizing his absence would give her more time to familiarize herself with her new life and get to know her daughter. Aubrey seemed like a sweet girl—though it was obvious she was a bit spoiled. It surprised Jordyn that in whatever absurd alternate reality she was living in, she'd become the sort of parent who let others raise her precious child.

After assuring him she'd be fine and he should go about his day, Kane left the house. Truth be told, Jordyn was far from fine, but she needed some time to herself to figure out what was going on. And, if her situation ended up being permanent, she needed time to explore what her new life held.

When Frida announced she was taking a trip to the grocery store, Jordyn jumped at the chance and offered to come along.

"That's not necessary," the housekeeper assured her.

"No, I'd love to get out. I could use the fresh air."

"Very well," Frida said. Her hesitation was thinly veiled. "Aubrey doesn't have preschool today but I could ask Mr. Davis to look after her while we're gone."

Jordyn had been relieved that Mr. Davis was still employed at Masters Manor. She'd always liked him. And she was equally relieved that instead of having to put up with Tiffany like Molly had, she had Frida as her housekeeper and nanny. The woman seemed far more suited for the job.

"No, that's okay," Jordyn said in response to Frida's offer. "We can take her with us."

"To town?" You sure you're up for that?"

"I think we can handle a four-year-old in town," Jordyn laughed, trying to understand the skepticism.

The housekeeper offered a tight smile. The look in her eyes suggested she had her doubts, but instead of conveying them, she said, "Of course, ma'am."

As they drove towards the store, Jordyn started to understand Frida's hesitation. Getting out of the house was its own fiasco. Aubrey fought with Jordyn and Frida over every detail—her shoes, her outfit, the location of her booster seat. But everything after the house was much worse. Aubrey repeatedly kicked the back of Jordyn's seat, despite several verbal warnings. She hollered when they didn't pull over to look for a dog she spotted trotting down the side of the road, and by the time they reached the grocery store she was screaming at the top of her lungs to get out of her booster seat. Jordyn felt a headache coming on. Frida was as patient as a saint but failed to mask her *I tried to warn you* expression.

Jordyn stepped out of the parked car, jerked open the door to the backseat, and leaned in close to Aubrey. "Now you listen here young lady," she said sternly, waiving a finger in Aubrey's direction but keeping a cool head. "This is no way to act. Now, we're going to go into this store. You're going to hold Mommy's hand and be a good little girl. If you do not, you won't be able to come to town with Mommy again, do you understand?"

"Yes, Mommy," the bright-eyed girl said sweetly. Her pretty little curls swept across her plump cheeks as her lips formed into a pout.

Jordyn unbuckled her daughter and took her by the hand. She squared her shoulders and led Aubrey through the front doors of the family grocery store, with Frida in tow. She felt smug satisfaction about how she'd turned the situation around. She thought to herself that she might just be a natural at this parenting gig.

Her satisfaction was short-lived. The moment they reached the center aisle, Aubrey's eyes fastened on the candy rack and she began to demand a chocolate bar. When Jordyn told her *no*, she started to howl, then took off running down the aisle.

Jordyn rushed after her but her daughter was quicker. She disappeared around the end of the aisle. When Jordyn rounded the corner, a man was crouched in the aisle so he was at eye-level with Aubrey. He wore a brown felt campaign hat and Jordyn's heart started to pound. As she came closer, she knew she'd recognize that calm, commanding tone anywhere.

When Brody saw her, he stood to his feet and tipped his hat. "Looks like you've got your hands full today."

She blushed. She didn't know how to feel. Awe, that Brody was so good with the unruly child. Sorrow that he didn't recognize her as his fiancée. Perhaps guilt that she was with Kane, which felt like a betrayal to Brody but a second chance to have everything she wanted. A marriage, a comfortable life, and a houseful of kids.

"It's good to see you, Sheriff Brody." She meant it. It was good to see a familiar face.

He smiled. Jordyn couldn't help but notice he looked shy. She recalled him being incredibly shy when she'd first met him. It was one of the things that had intrigued her about him. How a mountain of man with such stunning good looks could be so timid. Later she learned his shyness seemed only reserved for her. It took going on three or four dates before she had him opening up to her. After that they'd been inseparable. And blissfully happy. At least until recently.

"It's really great to see you," he said, interrupting her thoughts. "How have you been?"

The concerned, quizzical look on his face made Jordyn think there was something deeper to his question but she simply smiled and told him everything was going great.

"How about you?" The small talk felt so unnatural given their history.

"Can't complain," he said. His gaze met hers. His eyes were kind—but more guarded than she was used to. He seemed to be studying her.

She shifted from foot to foot under his stare. She wondered if he noticed the bruise on her forehead she hadn't bothered to cover up. She figured she should explain it to him, but since she couldn't recall her fall, it didn't seem like her story to tell.

It appeared Brody was about to say something else when Jordyn broke in with, "Well, we won't keep you." She secured Aubrey by the hand then said, "Have a good day," as casually as she could manage.

The sheriff tipped his hat again and turned to go.

As he walked away, Brody was unaware that Jordyn's eyes and thoughts were on him. She was quietly telling him goodbye.

Despite how hard he would try Brody knew he wouldn't get Jordyn out of his mind for the rest of the day. The chance encounter had been bittersweet. Over the years the spirited gleam in her eyes had diminished but she hadn't lost her overall shine. Her smile might have been forced but the bruise above her eye was real enough. He liked to see her. Didn't like to see her like that. It wasn't his business, he reminded himself. Jordyn was a strong woman. And she'd made it clear long ago she didn't need him, or his interference. Reluctantly, he'd granted her that wish.

"I ran into Sheriff Brody in the grocery store today," Jordyn told Kane over dinner. They were enjoying a quiet, candlelit dinner for two in the dining room. After preparing an impressive meal of roasted chicken, new potatoes, and asparagus, Frida had fed Aubrey an early supper and was upstairs giving her a bath.

Kane scowled and took a swig of wine. "Snooping into everyone's business, no doubt."

"Hey, Brody's done a lot for this town," she defended.

Kane set down his wine glass with a thud, which made Jordyn jump as red wine sloshed over the rim and landed on the white linen tablecloth. Then he took a deep breath and skimmed his hand over his fork. "My apologies," he said, offering her a lopsided grin. "I'm a bit of a grump this evening."

He wiped his mouth with his linen napkin, then stood up from the table and crossed to where Jordyn sat. He knelt beside her, placed a hand on the back of her head, then drew her in for a kiss. The image of Brody popped into her head along with a small pang of remorse. But the guilt she felt was quickly replaced with a deep longing. A longing for Kane. Her arms circled his neck and she returned the kiss.

"I've missed you," she found herself admitting.

He scooped her up from her chair as he continued to crush his lips to hers. "I think we can remedy that," he growled seductively as he carried her down the hallway towards the master bedroom.

Chapter Twelve

"Just order both," Kane teased Jordyn when she mentioned she was torn between the prime rib and the duck. He'd surprised her by taking her to a fancy restaurant about twenty minutes out of town. It was a place that usually required reservations months in advance, especially for a Saturday night, but his clout got them in immediately.

Jordyn rolled her eyes at his suggestion, knowing she'd never get used to not having to worry about money. She and Brody had always done alright for themselves but going to a restaurant like the one she and Kane were at would be a rare occasion. And ordering two entrées at once. Unthinkable.

She chose the prime rib, unable to bring herself to order both despite Kane's insistence. But he surprised her by also secretly ordering her the duck.

"Ugh, I can't eat another bite," she said, clutching her stomach and pushing both plates away from her. She'd done her best to finish both courses, but despite her valiant efforts, she was destined to have leftovers.

"You're going to have to hit the gym equipment extra hard to work off that meal," Kane teased.

Jordyn smiled, although she had no plans to work out later. Or maybe ever. "Thank you for tonight," she said. "This restaurant is so incredible."

He reached across the table, taking her by the hand. "You're incredible," he said, giving her hand a squeeze.

She blushed at the unexpected compliment.

Despite the cold, when they left the restaurant, they both felt warm from the wine.

"Let's take a walk through the square before we head home," Jordyn suggested, knowing they were both unfit to drive and not wanting their evening to end. Town square boasted a beautiful park with a gazebo and a covered carousel. Jordyn had always been a romantic—and thought the setting was perfect for her first real date with Kane.

He held her hand as they strolled past people and streetlamps. It was getting the late and the streets were emptying out. They stopped to rest on a park bench. The metal bench was cold, and Kane scooped her into his lap and held her close.

"Love you, Jordie," he whispered in her ear.

"Mmm," she mumbled contentedly, loving the moment but unable to allow herself to say those three little words. At least not yet.

After an incredible evening, Jordyn was convinced her life couldn't be more perfect. Wanting to hold onto that feeling, she hid her disappointment when, after they'd made love, Kane received a phone call, then announced he was going out again.

"Unexpected business," he'd said, as if his sudden departure wasn't out of the ordinary. Then he'd kissed her on the forehead, mumbled something about his absence giving her a chance to get in a workout, then left without further explanation.

The evening's sudden turn left her disoriented. Feeling abandoned and more than a bit miffed, she passed the workout room. She stepped inside, glared at the equipment, then shuffled to the kitchen instead where she poured herself a glass of wine. Then she stomped to the living room, bringing both her glass and the bottle with her.

Chapter Thirteen

"I'll be off early for the appointment today," Kane told Jordyn as he grabbed his to-go mug of coffee and prepared to leave the house. He seemed so different from the loving, patient person he'd been over the weekend. Now he acted cross and like he was in a rush to be somewhere. And, as usual, Jordyn had no idea where that somewhere was.

She racked her brain for whatever appointment Kane was referring to.

"The well-check appointment. For Aubrey," he said in reaction to the blank look on his wife's face. "The reason we gave Mr. Davis and Frida the day off today and why Aubrey's not in school this morning." His frown and patronizing tone suggested he thought Jordyn was failing at her parenting duties. Or perhaps she was projecting her own self-doubt and insecurities and was reading too much into her husband's expressions.

"Oh, right, the well-check. Will you be coming home so we can drive in together, or should I just meet you there?"

"I'll just meet you there."

Jordyn frowned.

Reading her expression as disappointment, Kane asked, "Why? Did you really want to drive in together?"

That wasn't it at all. The problem was Jordyn had no earthly idea where the appointment was at and at what time. If she asked, she'd have to admit just how little she remembered of their lives together. She got the impression Kane wouldn't understand. Then again, who would? She imagined herself trying to explain. *Sorry, I'm not supposed to be married to you. I'm actually supposed to be in a committed relationship with the town sheriff whom you hate. I have no memory of giving birth to our daughter or of our lives together until about a week ago. Any questions?*

"Jordyn?"

"Yes?"

He sighed, impatiently. "Did you need me to come home so we can go in together?" It was evident by his tone he had no intention of coming home prior to the appointment.

"No, no. Sorry, I was just thinking. I'll meet you there." She smiled, then crossed the room to throw another log into the fireplace. She wasn't cold. But she needed something to distract her from Kane's pitying stare.

Once her husband left the house, Jordyn frantically searched for clues to the location of Aubrey's appointment. And the time. She thought about calling Frida or Mr. Davis on their much-deserved day off but thought better of it. Determined to find the information on her own, her first instinct was to check the refrigerator. It was loaded up with Aubrey's artwork, her school pictures, a couple of wedding and baby shower invites, some assorted magnets—but no family calendar. No appointment cards.

She thought of the calendar on her phone. She plucked her cell from the counter, scrolled to the calendar app, but nothing was entered for that day. She did notice she had a fundraiser committee meeting at the townhall coming up. That fact did make her smile. It was nice to see something that hadn't changed from her past life. In the world she used to know, she'd chaired the committee. She hoped she still played an active role.

Her next move was to grill Aubrey about who her doctor was. She wandered upstairs into her daughter's playroom and found her having a tea party with an assortment of dolls and stuffed animals.

"Hi, sweetie," Jordyn started in. "Can I join your tea party?"

Aubrey's eyes lit up. "Sure Mommy. You can take Dolly's seat." She removed a doll from one of the plastic chairs and patted the seat, inviting her mother to sit down.

Jordyn was thankful for her young knees and back as she squeezed herself into the tiny chair that wasn't designed for anyone older than six. Despite her thin frame, she felt the chair creak under her weight. "So, looks like you have a doctor appointment today," she said, not knowing where to start.

She thought her statement was benign, but the reaction it incited in Aubrey took her by surprise.

"No shot," her daughter screamed. "I don't want a shoooooooot," she howled at the top of her tiny lungs.

"Aubrey, no, no. Shh." Jordyn scrambled out of her chair, wrapped the little girl in her arms, and kissed the top of her head. "No shot, I promise." She actually had no idea if her daughter was due for a vaccination and hoped and prayed she hadn't just lied to a four-year-old.

She sat through a couple imaginary cups of tea before excusing herself to go downstairs and start lunch. In actuality, she needed to get back to her search for the place and time of Aubrey's appointment.

After rummaging through junk drawers, a stack of mail, and even the glovebox of her SUV, her search proved unfruitful. She was reduced to tears. What sort of mother doesn't know the name of her own child's doctor? She sat down at the kitchen bar and took a breath. *Think, Jordyn. Think.* Then an idea popped into her head. Since the day she and Brody had decided to try for a baby, she'd been researching the best pediatricians that Sugarcreek and the neighboring towns had to offer. Dr.

Farnsworth. That was who she had selected after several months of deliberation and glowing references.

She dug her cellphone back out of her pocket and conducted an internet search for Dr. Farnsworth. Her palms were sweating as she dialed his listed office number. *Please, please,* she said aloud as the phone rang. Once. Twice. Then someone picked up.

"Dr. Farnsworth's office. Jessica speaking. How may I help you?"

Jordyn gripped the corner of the countertop and silently prayed her hunch was correct. "Hi, Jessica. This is Jordyn Reilly. Sorry, Jordyn Masters."

"Oh, hello Jordyn. You and Aubrey going to make it in today?"

Thank you, Lord, Jordyn mouthed quietly to herself. Then she said aloud, "Oh, yes, but I don't seem to have entered the appointment time into my phone. Could you remind me when it is?"

"I believe it's at one-thirty but let me confirm." She heard the clicking of a keyboard, then Jessica said, "Yes, one-thirty. Will that still work for you?"

"Yes, perfect. I'll see you then." When she hung up the phone, she burst into tears. Part relief. But mostly frustration at realizing that if she truly was stuck in this life for, well...life, she was going to have to continue to pretend to remember over a decade of events she wasn't ever truly party to.

"What's wrong, Mommy?" Aubrey's sweet voice interrupted Jordyn's crying spree. She realized she'd gotten lost in her own emotions and forgotten she had a child to take care of. A child she'd have to convince shortly to get ready and head to the doctor's office where she may or may not get a shot despite being reassured a shot was not on the docket for the day.

Guilt consumed her about being such a selfish parent. Whether or not she remembered giving birth to Aubrey and raising her to this point had no relevance when it came to taking care of her. It shouldn't be her daughter's concern whether Jordyn remembered. The fact was, Jordyn was her mother and was responsible for her daughter's care and upbringing. And up to this point she was failing on almost all parenting fronts.

She dried her eyes and smiled into the big, bright eyes of her daughter. "Nothing, sweetheart. Sometimes Mommy just has silly moments. I'll tell you what, let's eat lunch and if we can get you ready early, we'll stop and get you some ice cream before we head to the doctor's office. Sound good?"

Aubrey's smile brightened at the mention of the words *ice cream* but she scowled in response to visiting the doctor. She crossed her little arms in front of her chest and said indignantly, "No shot!"

"No shot," Jordyn agreed. She figured she'd need to have a private word with the doctor, or Jessica at the front desk, to let them know that if her daughter was due for vaccines, she'd need to make a separate appointment since she had made her a promise.

Despite several minutes of chaos while Jordyn searched for her keys and Aubrey threw yet another temper tantrum in reaction to Jordyn telling her she could only bring one toy with her to the doctor's office, they made it to the appointment with fifteen minutes to spare. And much to Jordyn's satisfaction, before Kane.

Her feelings of satisfaction morphed into annoyance once she had completed the check-in paperwork and perused the available magazines for twenty minutes or so. At closer to two, a nurse came out and invited Aubrey and Jordyn back to the exam room. Annoyance grew to concern once Aubrey had been weighed, measured, and the two awaited the doctor. It was now forty-five minutes past the start of the appointment and still no sign of Kane.

She tried his cell. No answer. She texted.

Worried about you. We're at the appointment.

After a few minutes, and still no response from Kane, the doctor came into the room.

"Hi, Dr. Farnsworth," Jordyn said, feeling a bit frazzled.

"Jordyn, how are you?" He held out his hand and she shook it. His handshake was warm and firm.

"I'm great," she lied. "How about you?"

"Well, you know me. Sheila and I have been hitting the slopes now that the golf courses are closed."

Jordyn smiled but didn't have much to add. After all, he was wrong. She didn't know him at all. And she knew even less about skiing.

"So, how is Kane?" he asked, switching gears. "Couldn't make it this time?"

Smiling thinly she said, "He must have gotten caught up."

Dr. Farnsworth patted her hand, then turned his attention to Aubrey. "And how about you, young lady? How have you been?"

Aubrey lit up at talking to the doctor. "I'm good. Momma said no shot today."

"Did she?" The doctor cast Jordyn a polite but questioning look.

She mouthed an apology and said, "I'll explain later."

The kind doctor winked knowingly at her. Then, refocusing his attention on his young patient, he said. "Okay, Aubrey. No shots today. Let's take a good look at you though. Can you stick out your tongue for me?"

Once the appointment was over and Aubrey had been given a clean bill of health, she and Jordyn headed back home. Aubrey sucked happily on the lollypop Dr. Farnsworth let her pick out from the prize basket. Jordyn had a death grip on the steering wheel as she drove. She stewed in silence as the mile markers passed by in a blur. Kane had texted while they were still at the doctor's office. Only a few brief words.

Something came up. Can't make it.

That was it. No other explanation. *Well he'd better have a good explanation when he gets home*, Jordyn fumed.

But the explanation didn't come. By the time Kane stumbled Into the bedroom, it was after two a.m. Jordyn could smell the liquor on his breath. It clung to his clothes and wafted through the room. Her stomach jolted in disgust. At the smell. At him in general for the way he'd been acting. But she kept her eyes squeezed shut and chose to pretend to be asleep. The path of least resistance. She was unwilling to accept she may have made a mistake when she put her faith and future in Kane's hands.

Chapter Fourteen

"It's family game night tonight," Aubrey announced excitedly as she bounded out of bed that morning. Her soft curls bounced atop her head as she skipped excitedly around her bedroom.

"Tonight, huh?" Jordyn asked, caught off guard and trying to wrangle the nightshirt off her daughter's head so she could get her dressed.

"Yes, every Tuesday Mommy," Aubrey reminded her, putting her little hands on her hips.

"That sounds like fun." This was news. "What is the plan for tonight's family game night?" Jordyn tried to phrase the question so it didn't sound like she hadn't been aware of the family tradition. Which of course, she hadn't until that moment.

"We play games. I get to pick the dessert."

"That sounds like fun." Jordyn perked up. She enjoyed board games.

Despite the long hours Kane worked and the nights he came home late, when he strolled through the doors that evening at 4 o'clock on the dot, it was obvious to Jordyn that he made Tuesday family game nights a priority. The thought softened her.

Like the dessert, Aubrey had the honor of picking the games. A treat for her. A bit of a trial for the adults, Jordyn quickly learned. The family played Hungry Hippo, Operation, and Battleship. Then, once Aubrey grew tired of the traditional games, the family suffered through games she made up on the fly. And often changed the rules as she went along to ensure she won.

"Cheater," Kane teased.

"No, Daddy, the rules always change in the second round."

He laughed and kissed his daughter atop her head. "Okay. What are the new rules for round three?"

Aubrey paused, considering. "It's a surprise," she finally said.

"I'll bet," Kane said, casting an amused wink in his wife's direction.

Once they'd exhausted their game options, the family gathered around the island in the kitchen to enjoy Aubrey's dessert of choice. Tonight's dessert was ice cream sundaes. Frida had bought all the toppings earlier in the day. Hot fudge, caramel sauce, assorted sprinkles, and cans of whipped cream lined the countertop. The housekeeper had filled pretty glass jars with gummy worms, gum drops, and Maraschino cherries. To make room for all the toppings, Jordyn picked up the vase of flowers that had been delivered earlier that day and set it on a nearby countertop. It was a beautiful arrangement of white roses, winter berries, noble fir greenery, and pinecones.

"Those are new," Kane observed.

"You're kidding, right?"

"What do you mean?"

"I mean, they're from you. At least I assumed they were. They didn't come with a card now that I think about it."

"They're not from me," he admitted.

"But when I called you earlier to thank you..."

He smiled devilishly. "I assumed you were thanking me for this morning."

She blushed. "Hmm..."

"Ice cream, ice cream," Aubrey chirped, growing impatient.

"Okay," Jordyn laughed. "Ice cream it is." The mystery of the flowers temporarily forgotten, she set out the ice cream and spoons for the toppings and the family dug in to build their own custom sundaes.

Kane chose vanilla ice cream and a single squirt of whipped cream. It seemed unimaginative to Jordyn, who instead took Aubrey's lead and used every topping available to her. Between the ice cream, whipped cream, and all the candy, by the time she put the final cherry on the top, her sundae looked about a foot tall. Ignoring Kane's look of disapproval, and subtle jab he made about the dessert going straight to her hips, she picked up a spoon and dug in before her dessert had a chance to topple over. She figured she'd have an ice cream headache and a sugar rush in her near future, but she hadn't had a sundae like that in years and planned to enjoy every bite.

It turned out to be Aubrey who suffered from the sugar rush. She skipped through the hallways, giggling and all but bouncing off the walls. Then, after a whirlwind of energy, followed by a momentous temper tantrum over brushing her teeth, the sugar rush turned into a sugar crash. The exhausted little girl fell asleep at the bottom of the stairs. Kane scooped her up and carried her to her bedroom. Jordyn joined him to tuck her in, then the two retired downstairs to the master.

After such a pleasant evening Jordyn had renewed hope in the life she was building with Kane. But once they reached the bedroom, his mood soured and her optimism started to fade.

"Nice cover with the flowers," he brooded.

"Pardon?" She was taken back. Her husband's volatile moods were something she wasn't sure she'd ever get used to. Unlike Brody, whose calm, stable demeanor was always a source of comfort. A comfort she'd taken for granted.

"You had to know the flowers weren't from me."

"Why would I have any reason to believe they weren't from you?" She searched her memories from when they dated in high school. Was he not the type to purchase flowers? Was he allergic to them?

His fists clenched and unclenched at his sides. "Are you trying to pick a fight?"

Wide-eyed, she stared over at him. Picking a fight was the last thing she wanted to do. She sucked in a breath and let it out slowly. "Kane, I really have no idea where this is coming from."

He glanced over at her. Saw the tears and genuine confusion etched on her pretty face. Then his scowl transformed to a look of concern. He reached for her, pulling her close and running his thumb across her forehead. The bruise had disappeared but he wondered how much damage that knock to the head had done.

"You sure everything's okay with you?"

"I am still having some problems with my memory," she admitted for the first time. Her bottom lip trembled.

He cradled her face in his strong hands. The charming, patient man she longed for returned. "Oh, honey, why didn't you tell me? I told you I'd take you back in for a CT scan if you needed."

"Because it's embarrassing." Her voice shook and a tear rolled down her cheek. She felt a whirlwind of emotions, but most of all, she felt relief. Relief that she could finally share at least a part of her secret.

"How much memory loss?" He searched her eyes for the truth.

She bit her lip, not sure how much to reveal. "A great deal, from what I've gathered. A great deal about us." She paused. "About Aubrey."

He nodded. "I see."

If she didn't know better, she'd think it was relief she saw on his face. "I couldn't even remember the name of Aubrey's doctor yesterday," she wailed.

"Oh babe, no wonder you wanted to drive in together. I'm so very sorry. I didn't realize. Here, come sit." He led her to the bed and sat beside her, holding her hand in his.

Jordyn wanted so badly to believe her husband was the caring, loving man he was portraying. Despite glimpses she'd witnessed that suggested otherwise. "Were we happy?" she asked, her voice hopeful. "I mean, are... Are we happy?"

He grinned. "Very." He pulled her hand to his lips. He kissed her knuckles, then her lips. "We're very happy."

She smiled. She didn't fully believe him. But the idea of the two of them being blissfully happy was a lovely sentiment.

Chapter Fifteen

"**P**retty flowers," Frida said the next morning. "From Kane?" Jordyn sensed there was more to the question than just idle curiosity. Not only that but Frida had been giving her sympathetic looks all morning.

"He says they're not."

"Interesting." Her brow furrowed but she didn't say anything further.

"Spit it out, Frida," Jordyn said, only half joking.

"Oh, it's nothing. It's just that..." She paused. "It's not my place to say. I'm so sorry. I know you've mentioned you were having some memory troubles. Perhaps this is one memory worth forgetting."

Jordyn tried to recall when she'd told Frida about the gaps in her memory. She wondered if it was Kane who'd told her. She took a deep breath, burying the feeling of betrayal down deep.

"Frida," she spoke softly, almost pleading. "Please tell me."

Her housekeeper avoided eye contact and stared down at her feet instead. Then she looked around to be sure Aubrey wasn't anywhere around. "Kane used to, um—Well, there's no delicate way to put this. He used to step out on you. A lot."

The news stung but somehow wasn't a complete surprise.

"Go on," Jordyn said, mentally scooping up her wounded pride from the kitchen floor.

"And after he did, he used to send you these elaborate bouquets of flowers as his way of apologizing."

"I see." Now it was Jordyn's turn to be embarrassed.

"But he's changed," Frida soothed. "You two worked it out. Kane started going to church with you. You privately renewed your vows. His renewed commitment was one of the reasons you implemented family game night on Tuesdays."

Jordyn nodded, finally understanding Kane's dedication to the Tuesday night ritual.

Frida continued. "Kane promised not to step out on you anymore. In turn you asked that he never send you flowers again. You know, because of what they used to represent."

Head spinning with a clearer picture of her relationship with Kane, and at a loss for words, Jordyn took a seat at one of the bar stools in front of the kitchen island. "I think you might be right, Frida. Some memories are best forgotten." She smiled to mask the pain she felt inside.

"I'll fix you an omelet," the housekeeper offered, patting her hand affectionately.

"Frida, you are wonderful. Your kindness is something I promise to never forget."

Jordyn was having trouble processing everything her housekeeper had told her. Maybe Kane had changed. Maybe he hadn't. But she also couldn't fathom who could have sent her the flowers. She had bumped into Brody a couple times in town. Perhaps he had sent them. But as quickly as the thought came to her, she dismissed it. Not only was Brody not the type to have flowers delivered—preferring to do it in person—it was also unlikely in whatever crazy universe she was now living in, that Brody would have any occasion to send her flowers.

Frida was like a regular P.I. and made it her mission to figure out who sent the flowers. She called the local floral shop, but they weren't any help. The customer had paid cash, declined a personalized card, and hadn't left a name. The owner couldn't even recall what he'd looked like. Or if it was even a *he*.

"What about that adorable clerk at the grocery store?" Frida asked as she passed Jordyn in the hallway, dust rag in hand. "You know, the one with the glasses. He always gets all gooey-eyed when you're around."

Jordyn laughed. "Hardly." What she didn't want to admit is she had no recollection of the grocery clerk whom Frida was referring to.

"Maybe it's a customer appreciation gift from one of the shops I frequent."

Frida shook her head. "If that were the case, seems like they'd want the credit."

"True. Perhaps it's my hair stylist—apologizing for what she's done to my natural hair color."

The two women burst out laughing. Jordyn held her side and Frida's shoulders shook with laughter.

After wiping away her tears of amusement, Frida said, "Yeah, I've got nothing."

"Well then. I'm going to pretend it's my fairy Godmother and she just knew I needed a pick-me-up."

"And apparently, a little intrigue," the housekeeper said knowingly.

Chapter Sixteen

"**W**hat are you trying to pull?" Kane barked into the phone the moment Molly picked up.

She paused on the other end of the line, then with a honey-infused, Texas accent, said, "I don't know what you mean."

Kane exhaled sharply as he pictured Molly blinking her eyes with mock innocence. "You send flowers to my wife?"

Another pause, then she asked, "So what if I did?"

"Dang-it woman, you pull another stunt like that again and..."

She interrupted him before he could finish with his threats. "Well, you don't have to be so mean about it." From the other end of the line her red lips formed into a pout. Then her tone turned from pouty to flirtatious. "And to think tonight I was going to let you see me in that new nighty you bought me."

"Don't try and change the subject, Molly," Kane snapped, only mildly distracted. "I've made it clear to you, what we have is not to interfere with my marriage. Do you hear me? That includes sending flowers to my wife."

"Didn't she like them?"

"Don't play innocent. You know exactly what the flowers would have made her think."

"Oh, did I not send a card?"

Irritated with her ploy at playing dumb, Kane hung up on her. He didn't have the patience for games. He did have the patience, however, to make the long drive to Stillwaters Inn so he could enjoy seeing Molly in her new lingerie. He had spent a pretty penny on it after all. He grew hard as he thought of ripping the expensive red, lacey fabric from her body. He'd need to stop and get cash to cover the room. He and the hotel owner had an arrangement. Discretion was key.

Jordyn paced back and forth in the kitchen, considering what to do with the bomb Frida had dropped about the flowers. She'd tried to make light of it with a game Frida and she had successfully played. And she had to admit, she did enjoy a good intrigue. But once the staff had gone home and Jordyn was alone with her thoughts, her mind drifted to what the flowers might mean. Had Kane sent them, then denied it, remembering what they could represent? Was he having an affair now? He was gone a lot. She felt so confused. Part of her wanted to pretend the flowers were from Brody and let that be the end of it. Ignorance was bliss.

She put her elbows on the countertop and rested her head in her hands. She felt a headache coming on. She pressed her fingertips to her temples to try and massage away the tension. Of course what she was self-diagnosing as a tension headache could in actuality be the product of the second glass of wine she'd had that evening while she'd stewed over the flowers and wondered what Kane was up to.

"Want to watch a movie with me, Mommy?" Aubrey's sweet voice interrupted her thoughts.

She lifted her head and focused on her daughter. With a forced smile she said, "Of course, sweetie. What did you have in mind?"

"The doggie one." This did bring a genuine smile to Jordyn's lips. Aubrey had discovered a movie about a talking dog and she'd been watching it on repeat for days. Jordyn figured either of them could recite the movie word-for-word.

"Doggie movie it is," she said, giving in. "Mommy's just got to do one thing first, then I'll pop some popcorn."

Once Aubrey wandered off to grab the stuffed animals that would be her movie companions, Jordyn plucked the vase of flowers from the countertop, went outside in the cold, and threw the flowers into the trash bin—vase and all. Then she walked calmly back into the house, determined to forget the matter.

Chapter Seventeen

Jordyn stood in front of the bathroom mirror in her nightgown, staring at her reflection, and wondering if she'd gone crazy. It had been over a week since she'd awoken in this strange realm and she was starting to give into the idea that her alternate reality might be permanent. She doubted she could have dreamed up the mouthwatering Thanksgiving meal of turkey, cranberry sauce, and mashed potatoes with gravy she'd just wolfed down with Kane and Aubrey. Or fabricated the emptiness she'd felt once she realized there wouldn't be any other friends or family over to share in the scrumptious dinner—not even Frida, who'd worked so hard to prepare it. No, this world she found herself in was clearly not a dream that she would eventually wake up from. But she pinched herself hard, just in case.

"Ouch," she said aloud. She'd managed to leave a small welt on her arm but she didn't wake up.

"Everything okay in there?" she heard Kane say.

Plastering a smile on her face he couldn't see from beyond the bathroom door, she called out, "Everything's fine. You know me, just clumsy."

She lied. She seemed to do a lot more of that these days. She was also doing a lot more self-reflecting. This fairytale that she'd thought she wanted wasn't turning out exactly as planned. Several times she reminded herself that nothing, and nobody, is perfect, and that she needed to learn to adjust. To accept what she couldn't change.

The self-imparted wisdom didn't stop her from the constant list-making in her head as she silently compared her old life to this new one.

This morning's list was a comparison between Brody and Kane. More specifically, it was a list of everything Kane had or did that Brody did not.

Cons:

Can be condescending

Comes home drunk often

Moody

Pros:

Money

Big house

Powerful

She reviewed the list in her mind. Could she possibly be so shallow that at one time she'd convinced herself that Kane would be better for her?

Mentally, she burned the list. Then she started a new one. One that cast Kane in a better light and didn't unfairly compare him to Brody. One that didn't make her seem so shallow.

Good provider

~~Committed~~ husband

Passionate

Good father

In her head she scratched through the word *committed*. With Kane's frequent late nights, she couldn't be so sure how committed he was to their little family. She suspected if he had to make a choice between his wealth or his family, she might not want to know which one he'd choose.

But he did marry her, she reminded herself, which was more than Brody had done. Not that she was still comparing…

"Hey, everything okay in here?" Kane asked again, this time from the open doorway.

She nearly jumped out of her skin. "You startled me."

"I can see that," he said with a grin.

Jordyn turned from the mirror and faced him. He was devastatingly handsome. She didn't add it to the list because she knew it was superficial. But each time she stared into his gray-blue eyes it was easy to get lost in them.

Kane stepped into the bathroom and pulled her close. His lips clamped down on hers and her list was temporarily forgotten. Her heart pounded as he pressed her against the sink. His firm hands caressed her thighs. She moaned softly as he pushed her nightgown above her buttocks and slid her panties to her knees. When he dropped to his knees to pleasure her with his warm mouth, her head lulled back and her eyes closed. Her hands fisted in his thick, dark hair as she allowed herself to be swept away.

Passionate, she thought. Was that on her list? And would it be enough? As she neared her climax, at that moment she was convinced it could be.

Chapter Eighteen

With Kane off at work, Jordyn decided to brave town once again with her daughter, but this time, without the help of Frida. She knew she needed more practice when it came to parenting. When she picked her up at preschool, Aubrey didn't put up a fuss the entire drive to town so she rewarded her by making the candy store their first stop. She was happy that it remained in the same location.

"The fudge is wonderful, as usual Mrs. Peters," Jordyn said. Mrs. Peters smiled back but didn't say anything.

"Aubrey, would you like another piece?" It had been a risk bringing her daughter into town, but unlike their previous experience, Aubrey was displaying model behavior.

"No thank you, Mommy. Can we go to the toy store next?"

Jordyn was pleased to see *Tino's Toy Store* was also in the same spot with the same brightly colored sign. As usual, the window display was impressive. It boasted a miniature, snow-capped village with an electric train running through it. In one corner was a stunning Christmas tree with hand-painted ornaments. Beautifully wrapped packages, stuffed animals, and faux snow were displayed beneath.

"It's so beautiful," Aubrey said in her sweet little voice as she pressed her mittens against the glass and stared in wonder.

"Do you know what you're asking Santa for?" a deep voice spoke up from behind them. Jordyn jumped. Aubrey squealed with delight and whirled around.

"Mr. Sheriff, Mr. Sheriff." She was jumping up and down, her cherub cheeks pink with enthusiasm.

Brody chuckled and knelt down so he was eye-level with the little girl. "How have you been, Aubrey?"

Jordyn stood quietly by and admired Brody's gentle approach with her daughter. It struck her as odd that he seemed more patient with her than Kane did. She brushed the thought away, realizing it was an unfair comparison. It was probably easier to be patient with someone you didn't see on a regular basis.

"Good. Mommy's taking me shopping today. We had fudge."

"That's great. And have you been a good girl this year for your mommy?"

"Yes. Yes, I have." Then she paused and looked at her mother. "Haven't I, Mommy?" Her blue eyes shone with emotion.

Jordyn laughed and patted Aubrey's head. "Of course you have, sweetheart."

When Brody stood to his feet to meet Jordyn's gaze, she blushed. Her heart was hammering in her chest. It had been a while since he had made her feel so exhilarated. She really had started to take so many things about him for granted.

"How have you been?" he asked.

If they were still together, she would have teased him with an innuendo about her being on Santa's naughty list. Instead she said, "We've been good."

Her smile was tight. Strained. Not for anything Brody had said or done, but because she wasn't sure how to act around him. As much as she wasn't willing to give up on her new life with Kane, doubt was creeping in. Next time they were alone, if she kissed Brody, she wasn't convinced she'd feel guilty about it. But she also wasn't convinced Brody would let her, her being a married woman and all.

"That's good," he said. He was smiling, but his eyes didn't hold the warmth and passion Jordyn had once been accustomed to. They were still kind, to be sure. But appeared flatter, somehow.

It pained her. Crossly, she reminded herself it was she, and not him, who had wanted something different. She cleared her thoughts and was about to ask him about work, when he unexpectedly tipped his hat and said, "Well, I'd best be on my way. You two ladies have a pleasant day."

Without another word, he walked away at a brisk pace. There was so much more that Jordyn had wanted to say to him. Instead, she remained glued in place as she watched him fade from view.

Chapter Nineteen

That evening Jordyn ate dinner without Kane for the second time in a week. She listened to Aubrey prattle on about preschool and dollies while she mulled over her situation. At first, she'd been excited about her new life. A handsome husband. More money than she knew what to do with. A precious daughter. Beautiful mansion. Staff to do all the daily chores she hated to do herself. But the longer she stayed in her new life, the more she discovered it wasn't the fairytale she'd first thought it to be. Aubrey was a delightful little girl, but Jordyn had to admit she didn't love her. Not like she was her own. She missed her store. She desperately wanted to talk to Hailie about everything going on. And above all, her heart was filled with longing. A longing for the way she'd felt when she was with Brody. Even at their lowest point, she had still felt loved.

"Where's Daddy at tonight?" Aubrey asked.

"Don't speak with your mouth full of food," Jordyn corrected as nicely as she could. "Remember Daddy had to work late tonight."

Aubrey grew quiet.

"Aubrey, what's wrong, sweetie?"

Her daughter crossed her little arms in front of her chest and pushed her lips into a pout. "Daddy always works late."

"I know he does, sweetheart. He works hard to provide for us." At least Jordyn assumed he did. It still wasn't clear what exactly Kane did for a living. And wasn't he already loaded? Rumor was he inherited millions from his father, along with the ranch. What business required him to continue to work so late if he already had more money than he, or his family, could ever spend?

As Jordyn tucked her daughter into bed that night, she again wondered to herself when Kane would be home. With Frida and Mr. Davis already gone home, once Aubrey went to sleep, the house was going to be unbearably quiet. And lonely.

"Mommy, I want to sleep with Ellie. Can you find her?"

Jordyn scanned the shelves overflowing with stuffed animals. She felt panic. Her eyes narrowed in on a light brown teddy bear with a red bow. It looked like it had received its fair share of cuddling. She reached for it.

"No, Mommy. That's Muffin. Ellie the elephant, remember?"

Ellie the elephant. She might have guessed that. There on the second shelf was a big, gray elephant. It looked brand new. She plucked it from the shelf and handed it to her daughter, who took it in her chubby arms and hugged it close.

"Do you want me to read you a bedtime story?"

"That's okay, Mommy. Frida read to me before dinner." *Of course she did*, Jordyn thought to herself. She gave her daughter a tight smile and a peck on the cheek, then crept out of the room.

After changing into light pink, silk pajamas that were too fancy (and frankly too pink for her taste, albeit extremely comfortable against her skin) she wandered to the kitchen and poured herself a generous glass of wine. She thought she might enjoy it from the comfort of her back porch so she grabbed a throw blanket on her way out the door.

She took a seat on the porch swing, wrapping the blanket around her legs. The night air was chilly, and despite the smattering of bright stars glowing above her, she felt lonely. After draining the contents of her wine glass, she stared blankly into the night sky and it seemed to frown back at her. Then, without warning, a tiny star winked in her direction. Without thinking, she winked back. Then, feeling foolish, not to mention half-frozen, she stood to go back inside.

Returning to the warmth of her house, she padded to the reading room, remembering how much she'd coveted the room when it was Molly's. As expected, it was decorated in a similar fashion. She had, after all, designed the same room in both realities. Although it could be improved with some of the space-maximizing pointers she'd learned in interior design school, the room felt inviting. But as cozy as it was, she was ready to give it back. She plucked a book from the shelf and took a seat next to the fireplace. Mr. Davis always started a fire for her before leaving for the evening. She was spoiled. And growing incredibly unhappy.

As she read the pages of her book, her thoughts wandered to Brody. She tried without success to push him out of her mind. She missed his laughter. Missed his touch. She'd taken for granted how easy it was to talk to him. How she could share almost anything with him. Even though he had never said *I do*, she now realized he was more committed to her than Kane was in this volatile marriage she found herself in.

"Good book?"

Kane's deep voice startled her. She set the book down and looked up at him with as much patience and adoration as she could muster. "Not really," she said, offering her sweetest smile. She stood to her feet and returned the book to the shelf. It gave her a few moments to compose herself.

"You're back earlier than I expected," she said with more enthusiasm than she felt.

He smiled. It was the rugged smile that used to melt her heart. Now she questioned if it was even sincere.

He reached out his hand and stroked her cheek, then gave a strand of her hair a playful tug. "What can I say, I missed you."

His words softened her some. She stepped towards him and he wrapped her in his arms.

"I missed you too," she said. It was a partial truth. At a minimum, she missed the intimacy. Missed having another adult to talk to.

When Kane's mouth claimed hers, she breathed in his masculine scent and tried to channel the feelings she'd felt not so long ago. But just as she felt herself giving in, a different scent assaulted her nostrils. A woman's perfume. *Vanilla Ecstasy* if she wasn't mistaken. It turned her stomach. She shoved him backwards, then ran to the nearest restroom to vomit in the sink.

"Jordie, you are overreacting," Kane told her for about the tenth time. "*If* you smelled perfume on me," he said, planting a seed of doubt, "it was probably because of Mrs. Weatherly. You know how that old woman loves to give out hugs. I ran into her at the hardware store earlier today."

Jordyn glared in his direction, searching for dishonesty behind his eyes. She refused to be made the fool.

He touched her hair. Then her cheek. "Sweetie, seriously. I promise, there is only you."

When she made a face to convey her doubt, he pulled her close. "Nobody in this town could hold a candle to you. I promise, I'd never jeopardize that." He cupped her chin, forcing her to look at him.

"Okay," she said hesitantly.

"Okay?"

He stared at her in a way that suggested he only had eyes for her. When he softly kissed her lips, this time her smile was genuine.

"Okay, I believe you," she said again with a bit more enthusiasm. Perhaps her guilt over not being with Brody was clouding what she had with Kane. Maybe she was subconsciously looking for ways to sabotage things. Her expression turned contrite. "I'm sorry. I overreacted. It's just you've been gone so much lately…" Her eyes burned and the tears threatened to spill over.

"I know. And I'm sorry about that." He took her by the hand and they sat down together. He patted her on the knee. "This is my fault. I've been working too much and you've been here cooped up in this house. I'll tell you what. Tomorrow's Saturday and I just have to check in on a few things with the ranch. I'll come home early. Then you, me, and Aubrey will drive into town and spend the evening together."

"I'd like that," she said, feeling more upbeat.

Jordyn strolled through town square with renewed happiness. Despite the chill in the air, she felt warm. Aubrey held one gloved hand and Kane the other. Fresh snow covered the sidewalks. Christmas lights and festive music made the entire experience seem magical. The streetlights glowed with the coming dusk.

The local ice rink was bursting at the seams with skaters, bundled up in their scarves, mittens, and hats. Shoppers bustled all around, their shopping bags stuffed with the homemade cheeses, salsas, and novelty items the town of Sugarcreek was known for and that kept visitors returning year after year. Jordyn glanced up at Kane with a twinkle in her eye and the crowd of people seemed to melt away.

He stopped, removed his cowboy hat, and glanced down at his wife. "You happy?" he asked.

She looked up at his handsome, chiseled face and stared into his beautiful eyes. "I'm happy," she told him. She told herself she needed to stop living in the past. This new life had many things to offer if she would just embrace it—and stop letting her imagination run away with her.

When she saw Brody off in the distance, talking to a tall blonde and laughing at something she'd just said, she felt regret. But she pushed it way down deep. And as she passed a health food store that in another life was the location of *Homespun Goodness*, her happiness wavered for but a moment. She took a deep breath, gave Aubrey's hand a tight squeeze, and leaned into Kane. This was her happy place, she reminded herself. With her happy, perfect family. She had no right to ask for anything more. Or anything different.

Chapter Twenty

Aubrey fell asleep on the ride home and Kane gathered her into his strong arms and carried her inside. Jordyn followed closely behind, taking in the view of her beautiful husband and daughter, illuminated beneath the porchlights. Her heart was full.

After tucking Aubrey into bed, she and Kane curled up on the couch in the family room to watch a Christmas movie together. Jordyn laid her head on his broad shoulder and he kissed the top of her head. The evening in town had been perfect. Her husband had been so patient. He seemed so committed to strengthening their marriage. Their family. She drifted off to dream, feeling content and full of newfound optimism.

When a noise outside aroused her from her sleep, Jordyn awoke to find herself on the couch. Alone. She sat up, rubbing the kink in her neck.

"Kane?" she called out, trying not to be cross that he'd gone to bed without her. Disoriented, she fumbled around for the lamp switch. Once her eyes adjusted to the light, she noticed a piece of paper on the end table. It was a note from Kane.

Needed to go out on business. Be home soon. xoxo

Stunned, she read the note several times, trying to make sense of it. What business could Kane possibly have at this hour? And why is it that he couldn't devote a single night to her? Optimism wavering, and heart in her stomach, she shuffled off to bed alone.

She wasn't sure at what point during the night Kane returned, but by the next morning he was in a foul mood and claimed he was too tired to go with her to church. Jordyn considered going without him, but decided to stay home instead, hoping to spend some quality time with him. She ached for the tender, patient man he'd shown her he could be.

"Let's do a picnic in the park today," she suggested once she'd coaxed him out of bed with the big breakfast she'd prepared.

Picnics were something she and Brody had often done and enjoyed. She needed to find ways to make it work with Kane. She didn't think they were broken per se, but she'd seen enough to realize their marriage needed work. If not for them, for the sake of their daughter.

"It's freezing out," he said, dismissing the idea without looking up from his newspaper.

"I know," she said with as much enthusiasm as she could muster. She moved to the chair next to him at the breakfast table. "That's what will make it fun. We'll grab a couple cozy blankets. Bring some hot chocolate. Bundle up and stay close." She placed her hand on his inner thigh.

Kane hesitated, but didn't immediately turn her down, which gave her hope she might be able to convince him. He set down the paper and studied her.

"We could trade out the hot cocoa for some hot-buttered rum," she suggested.

"Why, because you think I need to drink during the day?"

He was surprisingly defensive. She inhaled sharply, desperate to salvage the moment. She wanted to point out he was already on his second Bloody Mary but she bit her tongue.

"No, of course not. I just thought that might keep us warmer. But you could fill that role." She sidled up closer to him and skimmed her fingers down his pantleg. She had to believe the tenderness remained between them. Hadn't he just shown her that side of him?

She could see him start to give in. At least a little.

"I have a lot to do today," he said.

"But it's Sunday." Jordyn felt like she was begging for his attention. She hated it.

"This ranch doesn't run itself," he reminded her. But after seeing the defeated look flicker across his wife's face, he said, "But I can try."

She nodded, but still looked disappointed.

"Hey," he said softly. He cupped her chin in his hand and smiled. "I'll try."

"Thank you," she said. But she didn't celebrate yet. His response was less than committal. And even if he had made her a promise, she was starting to learn he wasn't the best at keeping them.

Jordyn knew better than to count on Kane returning in time for a picnic, which is why she was so surprised when he returned in the early afternoon. Mr. Davis followed through the door shortly after, loaded down with newly purchased picnic supplies—a small cooler, blankets, assorted cheeses and snacks, plastic champagne flutes, and a bottle of champagne.

She felt a stab of guilt that her plan had caused Mr. Davis to have to run errands for Kane on his one day off a week, but the guilt was overridden by joy and surprise at seeing that the picnic was actually going to happen.

"You made it," she said, beaming.

Kane smiled at the way her whole face lit up. "I said I'd try."

She stepped towards him. "Thank you." She pecked him on the cheek. "Really, Kane, this means so much."

He stroked her cheek and kissed her softly. "My pleasure," he told her, truly meaning it. He wasn't daft enough not to see what was right in front of him. His wife was beautiful and patient and generous. Sometimes it took sacrifices to make things work. He'd indulge her little picnic, then he wouldn't feel so guilty the next time he came home late. He was a man, after all, he reasoned. Surely, she couldn't expect him to be tied down to only her for the rest of his life. He had needs. She fulfilled most of them. But not all.

After leaving their cellphone numbers with the sitter Kane had arranged to watch Aubrey, they drove Kane's truck up into the hills. The snow was deep, so they both bundled up in snow pants, ski jackets and fur-lined snow boots.

"Not too late to turn back," he teased her.

"It is pretty cold," she admitted. Despite the heat being cranked in the truck, the cab hadn't yet warmed up and she could see her breath as she spoke. She slipped out of her boots and put her socked feet up on the dash to try and warm them. A memory popped in her head of how Brody used to lecture her about putting her feet up on the dash in case the air bag deployed. His lectures in safety used to drive her mad. Now she understood more than ever that he did it because he cared.

She pushed the thought away and forced herself to focus on the present. "This is nice," she said. "I like the alone time with you."

Kane grinned. "Let's eat inside the cab. We can still spread out the blanket. Pretend we're sitting on the hard, cold ground if that's what you find romantic."

"I mean, how could I not?" she said with a nervous laugh. She hadn't fully thought her plan through. She was pleased Kane was making an effort but she wasn't entirely sure she and her husband had enough in common to carry on a conversation during a long picnic. She supposed they could always talk about Aubrey but that didn't seem appropriate for a date.

She was pondering all of this when Kane took her in his arms and kissed her. He buried his face in her hair and whispered in her ear, "I do love you, you know."

She nodded. She supposed he did in the best way he knew how. But he'd always love himself and his money more, which was the real problem. His business obligations almost always took precedence over his family. As much as Jordyn wanted to believe that it could, she was starting to believe that would never change.

Instead of returning his expressions of love, she kissed him. His lips were full and warm. She had to admit he was a good kisser. A little greedy, but she didn't mind. His large hands cradled her face and she closed her eyes. But when Brody's face popped into her head, this time she didn't brush the image away. She clung to it as tightly as Kane was clinging to her.

Chapter Twenty-One

"Can I ask you something?" Frida asked Jordyn one morning after they'd both returned from dropping Aubrey off at school. She looked timid for the first time.

"Of course," Jordyn replied, secretly hoping her housekeeper wouldn't ask a question that required her to recall anything from prior to her head injury.

"Are you no longer happy with my services?"

"What?" She was taken back. "No, of course not. I'm incredibly grateful to you and everything you do. You're like a godsend. Honestly, I don't know how anybody manages without someone like you." Jordyn almost cringed at her own words. She sounded like such a snob.

Frida cocked her head to the side, trying to gauge if her employer was being sincere or if she was placating her.

Sensing the hesitation, Jordyn said, "Truly Frida, I couldn't be happier. What brought this on?"

Forehead perspiring and cheeks a bit pink, her housekeeper said, "Well, it's just that you've started doing a lot of your own cooking. And I feel like you're having me spend less time with Aubrey. Are you sure I haven't offended you in some way?"

"Oh, no Frida. I'm so sorry. And it looks like it might be me who has offended you."

Frida smiled. "No. I'm not offended. I just want to make sure I'm doing a good job for you."

"Of course, of course. Please, take a seat."

The two women sat down at the kitchen island.

"Can I tell you a secret?" Jordyn asked. She wasn't sure yet if Frida was someone she could trust but she figured her housekeeper was as close to a friend as she had.

"Well, if it's about Mr. Masters, I'm not sure I should..." Frida glanced around as If she feared Kane mlght overhear her even though both women knew he was miles away in town. Jordyn was a little disappointed, getting a clearer picture of where her housekeeper's loyalties might lie.

"No, it's nothing like that," she assured her, although she didn't feel as up to talking as she'd felt moments ago.

"Oh, please don't get me wrong Mrs. Masters."

"Jordyn."

"Please don't get me wrong, Jordyn. I just feel like if Mr. Masters found out I was keeping secrets from him..." The pinched voice and wild look in her eyes revealed it wasn't out of respect for Kane that Frida wasn't willing to keep a secret from him. She was terrified of him.

"Hey, I would never ask you to do that." Jordyn reached across the counter and gave her hand a gentle squeeze. And she meant it. At least not now that she knew how scared she was.

"I promise, this secret isn't about Kane. Just about me. And it's really only a secret because I'm embarrassed about it."

The housekeeper smiled warmly. She relaxed her shoulders as the color returned to her face. "Well then, lay it on me."

Jordyn laughed. "Well, a couple weeks ago you may recall that I hit my head."

Frida nodded but a strange expression flickered across her face. Taking the silence as confirmation, Jordyn continued.

"Well, ever since I woke up, I can't recall anything about my life with Kane from before that day."

"Anything?"

"Anything."

"Aubrey?" Frida asked, eyes wide with shock.

Jordyn's eyes misted. "Afraid not."

"You should go to the hospital."

"No, I think it's more like karma." When her housekeeper gave her a puzzled look Jordyn said, "Never mind. Anyways, I'm trying to do more with Aubrey so I can rekindle whatever bond we might have had. And the cooking and baking…well, I guess I'm trying to get a feel for where I fit into all of this."

This time it was Frida who reached out her hand and gave Jordyn's a squeeze. "Thank you for explaining it to me. I'll help you get through this."

"I appreciate that, Frida. Truly." She felt warmed at the prospect of forging a true friendship.

"Well, no wonder you were so optimistic about taking Aubrey to the grocery store that one day."

Jordyn burst out laughing. "Yes, that trip was a real eye opener."

The two women sat in silence for a few moments—Jordyn sipping her coffee and Frida taking sips of tea. Then Jordyn said, "You know what would be fun? We should throw a party."

"A party?"

"Yeah, a fun Christmas party. We can decorate, make appetizers and desserts. Serve champagne. People can get all dressed up."

The housekeeper looked doubtful. "You want a bunch of strangers wandering around your home? People who you'll also have to feed and let drink all your alcohol?"

"It's called being neighborly," Jordyn laughed.

"More like being taken advantage of," she countered sternly.

"Did we really never throw parties before? This big house seems perfect for it."

Frida shook her head, *no*.

As Jordyn thought about it, she couldn't recall Kane and Molly throwing any either. They came to many of the local parties and charity events—but never opened their home to host a party of their own.

"I think it could be fun. It would give the two of us a chance to try out new recipes. Maybe get to know each other a little better."

"I'm not sure if Mr. Masters will go for it."

"I think I can convince him," Jordyn said, refusing to let anything spoil her mood. "Now c'mon, let's get to planning."

An hour later and the two women had made a guest list a mile long and an equally impressive list of appetizers.

"We may need to scale back on the guest list," Frida said.

"Nonsense. I've always operated under the rule of thirds. I figure on only a third of those invited actually showing up. With such short notice, many people will already have plans. Others will simply be too busy with Christmas shopping and giftwrapping to steal away for a few hours."

"Does that rule of thirds apply to this menu?" Frida asked, staring at the daunting list of appetizers, and not recognizing half the foods on the list. Bacon wrapped lobster tails, caprese skewers, and kielbasa bites she could get behind. And she thought she had a marginal idea of how to prepare them. But she drew the line at goat cheese ladyfinger crostini. And what the heck were phyllo bites?

"Okay, fine," Jordyn said, giving in. "We can slim down the list of appetizers. But the grilled polenta bites stay."

Kane was hesitant about throwing a Christmas party, but Jordyn was relentless in convincing him.

"Think of it as a preemptive strike in your plans to run for mayor. You could use it as an opportunity to gain favor with the locals," she said, easily batting down his final argument against the party.

He nodded, abruptly coming around to the idea. "I didn't realize you knew I planned to run for mayor."

"Well, I'm sure you must have mentioned it," she said. It was actually Brody who'd shared the news with her in another world that seemed like a lifetime ago. Complained about it, actually, but of course that fact was just one more thing about her past she couldn't share with her husband.

Once Kane was on board, party preparations commenced quickly. Mr. Davis was tasked with hanging extra Christmas lights and Frida and Jordyn got busy finalizing the menu and preparing the house to host a large gathering. Although Kane didn't do any of the work himself, he offered his support by hiring extra hands to move furniture to alternate rooms, polish the floors, and to help Mr. Davis hang the lights.

"Is our house magic?" Aubrey asked when she came home from preschool and saw the added lights and smattering of garland, ribbons, and poinsettias. Jordyn had even splurged on the trainset she and Aubrey had seen at the toy store just days before. It circled the tree and added an extra flair.

"A choo-choo train, a choo-choo train," Aubrey had said excitedly.

Despite Jordyn's insistence, Frida and Mr. Davis declined to come to the party—requesting the night off instead. Jordyn was disappointed, but she understood the affair might not be their scene. Honoring their wishes, she hired temporary help for the event instead.

"Is that what you're going to wear to the party?" Kane asked when Jordyn was trying on her gown the night before the big event.

"That was my plan. Why, don't you like it?" When she had found the black, floor-length dress in her closet, she'd thought it was one of the prettiest gowns she'd ever seen. Simple, but elegant.

Kane came closer, looking her up and down. "No, I think it looks nice. Probably just the whole package that's throwing me."

Jordyn did her best to mask her hurt when she asked Kane to clarify what he meant.

"Your roots are showing and your nails could use a fill." His tone wasn't cruel—but it strongly suggested he recommended she do something about it before the party.

Instinctively, Jordyn smoothed her hair, then glanced down at her nailbeds. Rather than start a fight, she added a trip to the salon to her long to-do list for the next day.

On the night of the party, armed with new color in her hair and a new set of nails, Jordyn felt prepared for anything. But she quickly learned the rule of thirds did not apply in a small town where the locals were dying to see the inside of Kane's grand estate. People flocked to Masters Manor wearing their finest evening attire. The parking attendants were working harder than expected and Jordyn slipped outside to let them know a large bonus awaited them if they could manage the unexpected guests. In hindsight, she realized she should have asked the guests to RSVP. A lesson learned should she throw another party.

Luckily, she hadn't skimped on the food. In addition to the hors d'oeuvres she and Frida had spent a full day preparing, they had given in and hired a caterer. Jordyn had used Kane's influence for the last-minute addition, but *Carol's Catering* from a neighboring town was only too happy to prepare a traditional Christmas meal of prime rib, ham, garlic mashed potatoes, cranberry sauce, and Brussel sprouts. For a price.

Kane had wanted to bring in a string quartet, but Jordyn thought that might make the party a bit too stuffy. She convinced him to allow her to play Christmas music instead. The classic Christmas songs played throughout the house at a high enough volume for the guests to enjoy, but not too loud where guests couldn't carry on a conversation without having to raise their voices.

Ding-ding-ding. A clanking of silverware against a champagne flute commanded everyone's attention. "I'd like to make a toast," Kane announced from across the room.

Jordyn stared over at him, curious what he might say.

When the guests quieted down, her husband proceeded. "I'd like to thank my wife for putting together this little soiree. It's nice to see everybody. We don't get many opportunities to see all of you and it really means a lot that you all took time out of your evenings to spend it with us. I hope you enjoy the food. And if you get a chance to try those little shrimp appetizers, they're my wife's personal creation and a mouthwatering treat." He stared over at his wife and raised his glass. "To Jordyn. An amazing wife. And amazing hostess."

"To Jordyn," the guests murmured enthusiastically, raising their glasses and smiling in her direction.

Jordyn beamed. Kane wasn't known for handing out praise publicly. Or at all.

Worried the champagne might be running low, Jordyn snuck into the kitchen to check on things. There she found the temporary staff she'd hired were busy popping champagne corks and wiping down flutes.

"Thirsty guests," Jordyn remarked.

The two men smiled knowingly but had been trained not to say anything that could be interpreted as speaking against the guests. Jordyn appreciated their professionalism and suspected they probably saw more in their line of work than most.

"If we do start running low," she said, "we have plenty of red and white in the wine cellar. We can open that up. I have a few boxes of stemless wine glasses down there as well."

Howard, the older of the two wait-staff nodded. "We'll discreetly come find you if that's the case, but I think what we have will hold out."

"Then again," Jordyn said, "I probably could have just served cold beer and pretzels with this crowd. I'm not sure why I tried to get all fancy."

This time her remark prompted a laugh from Howard. He turned to her in earnest and said, "I think it's really nice. People appreciate fancy every now and again."

Jordyn beamed for the second time that evening. "Appreciate that. And hey, even if we don't run out of champagne, find me afterwards. I'll send you each home with a couple bottles of wine. Your pick."

She hurried out of the kitchen to mingle with her guests before her absence could be noticed. Rounding the corner between the kitchen and the living room, she bumped into Brody. His presence in her house sent a shiver of pleasure down her spine.

"Brody," she said as casually as she could manage. "I didn't expect to see you here."

"Well, everybody was invited."

He sounded testy and Jordyn worried she might have offended him. The last thing she wanted was to make him feel unwelcome. "Oh, absolutely. I'm so glad you could make it. I just figured this whole thing wasn't your scene."

He smiled, his soft brown eyes studying her. "Usually isn't. I made a singular exception."

If Jordyn didn't know any better, she'd say Brody was flirting with her. And shamelessly. She felt herself blush. "I'm honored." She paused, swallowing hard. "We," she corrected herself. "We are honored."

"No, you had it right the first time." He stepped closer to her. "Is there one of those for me?"

"Huh?" Being so close to him made her head swim and she struggled to make sense of his question.

Brody pointed to the champagne flute in her hand.

"Oh, yes. Here, take it," she said, offering him her glass.

"No, don't worry about it. I can get the next one that comes out of the kitchen."

"Trust me," Jordyn said. "The champagne is running out and you do not want to miss it." She pressed the glass into his hand. Shivered at how it felt when her fingertips brushed his.

When Brody took a sip of the champagne, Jordyn studied his face for the slightest hint of dislike. Six years of being in a relationship with him and she knew all too well that he didn't care for it. And he'd tried all types. From the cheap bottle they drank on the one-year anniversary of their first date, to the *good stuff* the mayor would send over around the holidays. So when Brody drained his glass and revealed nothing but a smile, she could only draw two possible conclusions. One, he was going out of his way to be polite to her. Or two, she was making him nervous and the champagne was the only liquid courage readily available to him. Both notions pleased her.

"Jordyn? Does that sound right?"

Realizing he had asked her a question she hadn't heard, her thoughts came to a screeching halt and she snapped back to the present. "I'm sorry, what was that?"

"Am I boring you, Jordyn?" Brody teased. His eyes danced with humor. And unmistakable lust. Jordyn's heart did flip flops.

"Quite the opposite, actually," she admitted. "I was, I guess...caught up in the moment."

"And were we...having a moment?" He was smooth as honey as he toyed with her emotions.

The dimples on his cheeks made Jordyn want to melt. She tried to compose herself. She straightened her necklace, then stared into his beautiful brown eyes. "You tell me."

When the party was over, the last guest had been ushered off, and the hired help had gone home for the evening, Jordyn sank into the sofa. She kicked out of her black stiletto heels. Kane walked over, loosening his bow tie. He plopped down next her. Exhausted and admittedly a little tipsy, Jordyn rested her head on her husband's shoulder. He took her hand in his.

"Great party," he told her.

"It was, wasn't it?" She smiled with pride.

"It was a shame the sheriff couldn't stay."

She felt herself tense. "Did he leave early? I hadn't noticed." She kept her head rested on Kane's shoulder and concentrated on keeping her breathing patterns normal despite the emotions the mere mention of Brody's name stirred in her.

"Yeah," Kane continued. "He nearly bolted out the front door. It seems you had quite the effect on him."

Clearing her throat, Jordyn asked, "What do you mean?"

"I mean that moment you two seemed to share in the hallway." Kane's voice changed. Jordyn could hear the hint of suspicion and anger in his tone.

She raised her head from his shoulder and looked him square in the eye. For some reason she found it easier to lie to him. It was something she never could have done so easily with Brody.

"You, my love, are acting jealous and I can assure you, you have absolutely no reason to be." Her arms circled around his neck and she kissed him on the cheek. "Now shall we go to bed and make sure you see where my interests lie?"

She thought she'd seen lust in his eyes. But instead, he turned her down, telling her he needed to turn in because he had an early start in the morning. Jordyn played at being hurt. In all honesty, what she felt was relief. And a nagging feeling that her husband refusing her meant far more than what was on the surface.

Chapter Twenty-Two

Just as Tuesday nights were family game night, Jordyn also learned the first Thursday of every month was Kane's pool and poker night with the boys. The illegal poker game and other activities of debauchery (Kane's playful words, not hers) were held in the main pole building behind the house. Since Jordyn rarely saw Kane with friends—only business associates—she was curious who *the boys* were. She wondered how she could ask without giving away how little she knew about the past ten years she and Kane supposedly shared.

"So, who's all coming tonight?" she asked as she finished up the final touches on the tray of hors d'oeuvres she'd prepared.

"You know Frida would have done all of this."

She smiled. "Maybe I want to show off my culinary skills to you."

"Up until a few weeks ago, I honestly didn't know you even knew how to cook. Only how to eat." Although he was smiling, his comment had a condescending bite to it.

Jordyn's smile faltered but she let the insult go. "Usual crowd?" she asked, rephrasing the question and trying to remain cheerful.

"Just the old gang from school. Charlie. Johnny. A couple business associates. Usually Marv if he wasn't in the slammer for something he hasn't done."

Jordyn was startled at hearing Marv's name. And at Kane's proclamation of the man's innocence. She felt a pang of guilt knowing it was she who'd put the spotlight on him, which ultimately landed him in jail.

"Oh, and Brody," Kane said, interrupting her wandering thoughts.

Her heart skipped a beat and her delicate fingers stopped arranging the pretty lemon tarts she'd prepared. She hadn't seen Brody since the party and secretly wondered if he'd been avoiding her.

"You, um, invited the sheriff?"

"No, Brody Risdale. My banker. You think I'd invite the fool who put one of my business partners in jail?"

"Oh, right," she said as nonchalantly as she could manage. She took note of the term *my* banker as opposed to *our* banker. She was also leery that Kane referred to Marv as his business partner. As far as she knew, Kane didn't have part ownership in Marvin's Garage. She wondered if the admission was a slipup somehow. Evidence her husband had shady business dealings she wasn't privy to.

Pushing aside her annoyance and suspicions, she plucked a morsel of food from the tray. "Open wide. I need a taste tester." She popped the sample into his mouth, resisting the urge to shove it in further.

The air in the shop was thick with cigar smoke and the smell of beer, and Kane wouldn't have it any other way. "I'll see your bet," he said, "and I'll raise you." He plunked down his chips and stared across the table at his opponent.

"You're bluffing," his old schoolmate, Charlie, insisted. The cigar smoke was making his eyes water but he kept his gaze focused on Kane's face, searching for a tell.

Kane nodded. A single nod. "Perhaps. Try me."

Charlie was starting to look a little green around the gills. "Call," he finally decided.

To Charlie's dismay, it turned out Kane wasn't bluffing.

"Read 'em and weep," Kane taunted as he slapped his cards face up on the table. His lips spread into a taunting smile.

The color drained from Charlie's face. He swallowed hard, then grinned to give the impression the loss he'd suffered at the latest hand wasn't a big deal. His grin came out as more of a grimace, which was a more accurate reflection of how he was feeling. It meant nothing to Kane to lose that much money. It was like throwing spare coins into a wishing well. Chump change. Charlie, on the other hand, had scrimped and saved all month to bring a decent pot to the card table. Not out of any desire to see his old friend. He'd ceased to think of Kane as a friend for quite some time now. The man was a bully. A cheat. But he was also a means to an end.

"Oh, c'mon Charlie. I'll spot you some cash if you want to play some more." Kane's offer was more condescending than sympathetic.

Charlie cleared his throat. "Oh, no worries. I came with more to play with." He reached into his back pocket and retrieved his wallet. As he did, the image of his wife's face popped into his head. He could almost see her look of disapproval. Hear the warning in her tone. The remaining cash in his wallet was for groceries, diapers, and baby formula. He'd promised his wife he'd pick them up on his way home. Now, as he plunked the cash on the table, he could only hope his rotten luck that evening would turn.

Kane might not be a true friend to Charlie anymore, but Johnny Timmons was. Like Charlie, Johnny understood what it took to run in the same circles as Kane. As a small business owner, it was a necessary evil in a town half-owned by one man. One powerful, unforgiving man who wouldn't think twice about destroying someone's lifelong dream if it furthered his agenda. For most of the men huddled around the poker table, remaining *friends* with Kane kept them thinly shielded from any negative interference with their livelihoods. For now. Marvin, who tended to be a pushover and a bit naïve, hadn't been as lucky.

Johnny knew his friend Charlie was in a pickle. But he also knew Charlie had too much pride to admit it—or to take a handout. Johnny hadn't done too bad for himself against Kane. He enjoyed taking Kane's money, even if it was an inconsequential amount to him. It was a matter of pride, and Kane's pride was wounded anytime he lost a hand.

Everyone at the table knew Kane often cheated at cards, but Johnny was usually too smart for that. Plus, when it came to Kane, Johnny wasn't afraid to cheat a bit his own self. Especially for a good cause. And tonight's good cause was Charlie. He planned to help Charlie take Kane for all he had. At least all he had at the poker table. And others may not have figured it out, but Kane had a tell. And Johnny was all over it.

An hour later and Johnny had cleverly managed to get Charlie his money back and had made an impactful dent in Kane's poker chips. He would have stuck it to him more, but out of nowhere Kane asked him, "So, tell me, are you enjoying that discount on your office lease that I had city hall throw your way?"

Johnny recognized the question for what it was. A veiled threat. But he didn't break his stride. "Sure am," he answered, showing his hand to reveal a royal flush—happy to win one last hand before quietly pulling back the reins.

Although Kane lost a sizable amount, he won the final few hands, which left him in a good mood. "I think it's about time to call it a night, boys," he announced. "Can't ignore my beautiful wife too long."

"Speaking of your wife—" Charlie piped in.

"We weren't. You don't speak about my wife. Only I have that right." Kane leaned across the poker table, menacingly.

Red-faced, Charlie said, "Sorry, sir, I just meant…"

Kane chuckled and slapped Charlie on the back. "I'm messing with you, Charlie." But despite his smile, he didn't drop the condescending tone.

Charlie smiled tightly back. "I was just going to say these lemon tarts she made were delicious." He stuffed a morsel in his mouth, hoping the sound of his own chewing would muffle the awkward silence.

"Charlie's right, these are amazing," Johnny chimed in. "Seriously, why the heck do you need Frida when Jordyn can cook like this?"

"Because I need my wife to save her strength and talents for other things," Kane said crudely.

The men around the table exchanged an awkward, knowing glance. They typically tried to avoid talking about any of their wives since Kane took it to a level of disrespect and nobody had the nerve to call him out on it. Nobody but Johnny that is, but only if you talked about his wife. He figured it was up to Kane to stick up for his own wife—and all Johnny could do was not comment back when Kane was the one dishing out the innuendos about Jordyn.

"Well, we'd best be going," Johnny announced, leading the way for the other men to make their exit. "Thank you, Kane for your hospitality. We'll talk soon."

Kane stumbled back into the house, tipsy and in a feisty mood. He pulled Jordyn close and ran his hands down her hips and buttocks. "Let's go to bed," he whispered through slurred words.

His breath felt hot against her ear and Jordyn's stomach lurched at the stink of booze and cigars. She wasn't sure if she could get in the mood with Kane so inebriated and her so sober. She was searching for an excuse to refuse him when Aubrey came running out of her room, stuffed elephant in hand, and announced she was too afraid to sleep by herself. Her intrusion was Jordyn's salvation.

"I can stay with her tonight," she offered, doing her best to mask her relief.

Arousal wavering, Kane nodded and headed to bed. By the time Jordyn poked her head in to check on him, he was asleep above the covers, fully dressed, and snoring softly. She tiptoed in, left a glass of water and two aspirin on the nightstand, then snuck back out and climbed the stairs to share the twin bed with Aubrey.

Chapter Twenty-Three

Jordyn drove into town Friday evening for Sugarcreek's monthly fundraiser committee meeting, grateful at least one thing in her life hadn't changed. She was a committee member before, and it appeared she still was. Except in her life with Brody she chaired the committee. When she arrived at city hall and found Latrisha Braun, a local shop owner, stationed behind the podium, she learned that was no longer the case.

She took a seat at one of the round folding tables, feeling a bit out of place. Other than a few friendly nods, nobody much acknowledged her presence there and she gathered she didn't carry the crucial role she was accustomed to. She decided that needed to change. She loved the fundraiser committee. It was one of the places she gave her heart and soul to—along with her creative ideas and her best baked goods.

Feeling a bit out of sorts as of late, she hadn't gotten around to baking treats for tonight's meeting. But when she saw the table in the back with its pathetic assortment of store-bought cookies, she realized nobody was expecting her baked goods in this alternate universe. Another fact she figured she'd need to remedy.

"If you can all take your seats, I think we'll get started," Latrisha said, glancing down at her watch. Her nasally voice echoed off the walls of the half-empty room.

The remaining committee members filed in and took their seats around the tables. The members were most of the same faces she was used to seeing. A couple new locals. A few missing—noticeably, Hailie. Jordyn felt a wave of nostalgia and regret over that. She missed Hailie even more than she thought she would.

"Jordyn?" Latrisha's voice broke into her thoughts.

She whipped her head forward, giving Latrisha her full attention. "I'm sorry, what's that?"

Latrisha smiled. "I was just asking if you've had a chance to ask your husband about donating the hay bales as seating for Sugarcreek's Christmas Eve bonfire."

Jordyn furrowed her brow, wanting to remind Latrisha that Brody was her fiancée, not her husband, and to inquire why he would be on the hook for donating hay bales. Then she realized it wasn't Brody Latrisha was inquiring about. It was Kane. Kane would be on the hook. Panic set in. She had no idea whether it was something she'd discussed with Kane. Really, this was the first she recalled ever hearing about it. She glanced around at the expectant faces.

"Oh, of course. Yes. Yes, he'll do it," she blurted out. Then she secretly hoped her husband was as amenable as Brody at doing favors she'd volunteered him for. Brody always agreed graciously. She had a feeling Kane might take a little more coaxing.

"Great," Latrisha said. "Now onto the next order of business. We need some fresh ideas to raise funds for the bonfire. The bake sale was a success but the proceeds went towards the new Christmas wreaths on the streetlamps and the setup cost for the tree lighting ceremony. We need something more. Ideas anyone?"

There was some murmuring amongst the tables, then an elderly lady named Patty raised her hand. Jordyn recognized her as the owner of the pet supply store. "We could have a big rummage sale. Maybe hold it in the grange hall."

"That's an excellent idea," Latrisha said. "What else? Maybe something we can do in the grange hall at the same time?"

"We could set up a face painting booth for the kids," another committee member suggested.

"I love that. And I know just the person to volunteer for the job. What else?" She paused, looking around.

Jordyn shifted in her chair, uncertain why she was so nervous to speak up. But when it was clear nobody else was going to, she finally raised her hand and said, "What about an auction? But instead of goods, since those will be part of the rummage sale, what about..." She trailed off, starting to doubt her idea. Perhaps it was a little out there for her small town.

"Go on," Latrisha encouraged her.

She grimaced. "What about if we auction off the menfolk? You know, the highest bidder can have them for two hours for honey-do lists or what not."

Latrisha looked hesitant.

Patty looked excited. "Like changing out the fluorescent lightbulbs in my shop's vaulted ceilings?" she asked.

"Ooh...or painting the accent wall in my house that I've been begging my husband for a year to do," another committee member piped up. Within moments, the room was abuzz with ideas.

"Ladies, ladies," Latrisha said. "And gentlemen," she amended, looking over at Ron, the sole male committee member.

"What do you think about the idea, Ron?" Jordyn asked. "Too...sexist?"

Ron chuckled, causing his big belly to shake. "Ladies, if you want to put me on display and fight over which one of you gets to spend a few hours with me, and it's for a worthy cause, I'm all in."

"Well, it's settled then," Latrisha said, finally giving into the idea. "Jordyn will arrange for the participants."

"Oh, wait, what?" Jordyn asked, taken by surprise. She'd been quick to offer ideas but hadn't realized it meant she'd be signing up for executing against them. She wasn't the committee chair, after all.

"Well, of course we're going to need Kane," Latrisha cooed. "And if you can convince him, you can convince anybody. Check with the local shop owners. Oh, and of course the sheriff."

Jordyn's heart was racing. Not because she was worried about convincing Kane, although she knew that alone would be a challenge. But more because she'd have to talk to Brody in person. And beyond that, she'd need to convince him to auction himself off. Even when they were together, that type of favor would have required some needling. And her hands were a bit tied when it came to the needling she could do now that he was no longer her fiancée.

Despite her apprehension, she found herself saying, "Sure, Latrisha. I'll do it. No problem." Then she made a mental note to also ask Kane about the hay bales. She probably wasn't going to be very popular tonight.

"An auction, huh?" Kane asked. It helped he was in a playful mood, in part because of the beers Jordyn had pushed on him during dinner.

"Yes," she said, smiling sweetly. "Imagine how excited all the ladies will be at the chance to have you as their personal slave for a couple hours." She leaned in and kissed him on the mouth. "Of course, I may have to get in on the bidding."

Kane took her in his arms and kissed her back. "An auction, and hay bales? Seems like a strange combination."

"Well, apparently I told them weeks ago I'd ask you about the hay bales for the bonfire but it must have slipped my mind."

"It's a good thing you're pretty," he teased. But despite his playful words, he failed to mask his condescending tone.

"It's a good thing you're shallow," she returned with a laugh, pretending her words were only in jest.

Chapter Twenty-Four

With Aubrey at school three days a week, Kane off doing goodness knows what, and Frida and Mr. Davis responsible for the household chores, Jordyn was still trying to reconcile what it was she was supposed to do with her time. In the beginning, she'd taken full advantage of the downtime—binge-watching shows she'd never gotten around to seeing and reading some of the classics. Then she'd tried to help Frida but had gotten the sense she was only in the way.

Alone in the kitchen, and bored to tears, an idea came to her. She could focus her time and energy on baking platters of assorted goodies for the local shops downtown. She figured she could drive into town and drop off a tray at each of her favorite places. The lawn and garden store. The toy store (for Aubrey of course). Perhaps the precinct. She smiled to herself, thinking about the possibility of seeing Brody. She pulled a notepad and pen from a drawer in the kitchen and jotted down the assorted goodies she was going to bake along with an inventory of the necessary ingredients she'd memorized but wasn't certain if her new, fancy pantry housed. She added blueberry scones to the goodies list—halfway convincing herself that they were a necessary staple to any tray of baked goods and not because they happened to be Brody's favorite.

The fancy mixer on the counter made her smile. It was similar to the one she was used to, but the more expensive model she'd been too cheap to splurge on in another life. With money being no object, she figured the Jordyn of this new life probably didn't think twice about handing over the extra cash for the larger mixing bowl and three additional accessories.

She was surprised and relieved to find the pantry and fridge were stocked with all the ingredients she'd need—minus the cream of tartar, but she preferred using a lemon juice substitute with egg whites anyways. She turned on the surround sound and enjoyed the Christmas tunes that flooded the house. She rummaged in the cupboards and found a couple crisply folded, rarely used aprons.

She selected the one with the gray and white striped print and tiny, yellow flowers. Not the most imaginative apron, but it was pretty. She put it on, tied it behind her back, and slipped the piece of paper with the list of ingredients into the front pocket. By that point she was feeling in her element. She hummed along to the Christmas music as she transformed the kitchen into her own private bakery. And for probably the first time since she'd awoken in that bazaar life and beautiful-but-too-stuffy house, she felt at home.

Her hair was different, Brody noticed when Jordyn stopped by unexpectedly to drop off the tray of goodies. Usually combed and set with such precision. Today it was hastily pulled back and held loosely in place by a blue bandana with paisley print. He preferred this new style. She looked comfortable. Accessible. He tried to remind himself that she was anything but accessible. Married to a powerful man. Mother to a young child who wasn't his. But there were moments, moments when he stared into those pretty, green eyes, where he could forget all of that. Forget and pretend she was his. After all, he'd always be hers.

"Thank you for the desserts," he told her as he tried his best to right-size his grin. Being around Jordyn made him smile broader than the situation likely called for. He reined in his smile so he didn't appear deranged.

"You're welcome. I know how hard you all work these days. More tourists equals more crime."

He nodded but didn't respond. He was having a hard time getting his lips and tongue to work properly.

Brody's silence was unnerving and Jordyn found herself fiddling with the gaudy diamond wedding ring that weighed down her finger. At least five carats, by her estimation. She missed the elegant, one carat ring Brody had picked out for her. Simple. Beautiful. Exactly to her taste.

"So," she said, clearing her thoughts. "You have any plans for the holidays? Maybe going back to San Francisco?"

"Nah. Been trying to convince my mother and two brothers to come here again." He paused. "It's just too hard to go back there. I see my late wife's face at every turn." He felt his voice crack. Wondered why he was revealing so much to her.

Jordyn reached up and touched his shoulder. "I understand. I really am sorry about your wife. I know it must get harder this time of year."

He nodded. The way she stared into his eyes it was as if she knew exactly how he was feeling. He cleared his throat, unnerved.

"Everything go okay today?" Kane asked over dinner. He tried to sound casual, but his tone held a hint of something Jordyn couldn't quite discern. Concern, perhaps. Or suspicion.

Her eyes widened with innocence. "What do you mean?"

"Oh, it's just that one of my guys saw you at the police station today." He took a bite of his filet mignon, then returned his fork to his plate. "Imagine my concern." His tone was menacing. His anger, thinly veiled. He pressed his napkin to his lips, set it back down, and waited for her reply.

"Oh yes," she said as casually as she could manage as she silently instructed her heart to stop hammering out of her chest. "I was bringing the officers a platter of goodies. I've been in a bit of a baking frenzy." She kept her fork firmly pressed in her palm to keep her hand from shaking.

Not because she was afraid of him, exactly. But the thought that her husband might be having her followed caused her great distress. Evidence their relationship was more broken than she'd already imagined.

She continued with her explanation. "I also brought a platter to six or seven of the shops downtown." She looked up from her food and stared directly into his eyes. It was her attempt to convey she had nothing to hide.

"A baking frenzy, huh?" he said, relaxing in his chair. "What brought that on?" His charming demeanor returned and he took another bite of his steak.

Jordyn masked her relief. "I think it's going to be my new hobby," she stated proudly. She set the fork down, her nerves settling. She still wanted to ask if he'd had her followed, but she worried it would make her sound paranoid. Or like she had something to hide. *Did she?*

"Leave any desserts for me?" Kane cooed.

Jordyn smiled, but it wasn't her genuine smile. "I may have set a few aside for you." *Only if you tell me how you knew I was at the police station*, she wanted to add.

Chapter Twenty-Five

Jordyn knew things were eroding between her and Kane. The writing was on the wall. He'd tried at first. She had too. They'd both used her lack of memory as a reason to start afresh. But that could only work for so long. It was when Kane skipped family game night without calling that Jordyn knew something was inherently wrong with their relationship.

To the townsfolk they seemed like the perfect couple. The rich, handsome cattle rancher and his dutiful wife. Behind closed doors they were bitter and broken. Well, at least she was bitter. He appeared to take everything in stride and seemed to be getting his satisfaction elsewhere. He often worked late. Jordyn supposed burying himself in his work might be his coping mechanism. Perhaps he was as miserable as she was and they both needed to admit it, then talk through it. Maybe they could use a therapist.

When Kane finally did come home and they had a moment alone, she mentioned the idea of couples therapy to him.

"I'm not putting our marriage in the hands of some quack," he said, dismissing her idea with a wave of his hand.

She was taken back by how quickly he turned her down. "Dr. Keller is supposed to be fantastic."

"You mean, Barbara? Trust me, that woman has more issues than anyone who she's trying to *fix*."

Jordyn frowned, remembering how hard Brody had pressed her to go to therapy once he realized they could use the help. She felt guilty. It must have hurt Brody—her unwillingness to go with him. To try everything she could to make them work. Then, once she finally agreed to go, she'd pushed him out after only one session. She really was a fool. She supposed she deserved every rotten thing that happened to her. She'd done this to Brody, ten-fold.

"So what, now you're just not going to talk to me until you can have your way?" Kane's cutting words sliced through her thoughts.

Accepting the fate she knew she deserved, and no longer wanting to argue, she pasted on a smile. "No, sorry, my thoughts just ran away with me. You're absolutely right. We don't need to go to a therapist."

"Of course we don't," he said, putting an end to the conversation by kissing her on the forehead before wandering off to the kitchen to grab a beer.

"I'm sorry, Brody," Jordyn mouthed to herself as she watched Kane's retreating figure. "I'm sorry for everything."

Before she drifted off to sleep that night, Jordyn started to consider if she'd died in real life and this new reality was her personal hell. A hell where she was forced to live out a life that she had been so certain she'd wanted and that turned out not to be the red rose garden she'd pictured it would be. Each day Kane seemed more distant. Less patient. He worked constantly—at least that's what he claimed—but he never shared what he did. Jordyn was starting to think that if Brody would take her back (not that he'd know they had any sort of history) she would crawl on her knees across the Colorado Rockies to make it happen.

Chapter Twenty-Six

Jordyn made the long drive to Molly Hauser's house. The longer the gravelly road stretched into the distance, the more she worried her GPS was leading her astray. It had been a surprise when Molly had called her that morning, asking if she could meet her. Jordyn wasn't certain if she and Molly were friends in this new world that was her current reality. She certainly hadn't heard from Molly in the time she'd been with Kane. Still, she felt awkward when she asked for her address. Based on Molly's lack of surprise by the question, Jordyn confirmed what she'd already suspected. That she and Molly didn't run in the same circles.

When Jordyn pulled into the drive, she felt a wave of regret. She was having a lot of those lately. About as often as a woman going through menopause has hot flashes. Back in the *real world*, Molly lived in a grand house and lived a life of luxury. She seemed happily married, had two beautiful children, and a baby on the way. Now, in whatever messed up reality they found themselves in, Molly lived alone in a single-wide trailer that was crumbling around her. A sagging porch. Snow packed roof lined with tires. Peeling paint. The place was beyond rundown. A massive branch from an old oak tree stretched over the rooftop, posing a dangerous threat if there was ever a powerful windstorm. There was no question the large tree branch would mark the end of the dilapidated trailer if it ever fell.

She did notice the deluxe, white SUV in the driveway and was happy Molly at least had a nice vehicle. But the upscale automobile seemed out of place next to the aging, single-wide trailer. Jordyn had never thought of Molly as overly vain, so it surprised her that she would spend her money on a fancy rig to drive around town as opposed to a nicer roof above her head.

Jordyn stepped gingerly as she ascended the rickety porch steps and walked to the front door. The deck slats creaked beneath her feet. She reached for the doorbell, noted the black, burnt smudges surrounding it, and opted to knock on the front door instead. She heard shuffling, followed by a *be there in a sec*. Within moments she found herself standing face-to-face with Molly.

The woman before her looked vastly different from how Jordyn was used to seeing her. Gone were the designer suits and platinum hair. Molly's hair was a rich, auburn color. She wore it long. Almost to her waist. It was pretty. Her clothes, however, left a bit to be desired. Rumpled. Nearly threadbare. It didn't take a detective to see Molly was struggling financially.

"I'm just tickled you agreed to come see me," Molly said with the thick, Texas accent Jordyn remembered from high school. That part did make Jordyn smile. The southern accent was more suiting.

Molly invited her in. The humble home smelled of mildew and carpet deodorizer. Instead of masking the smell of the potential mold problem, the floral fragrance of the deodorizer hung in the air, heightening the unpleasant odor. Jordyn's throat felt thick as the sickening combination of musty and sweet assaulted her nostrils and lungs.

The two women took their seats in the living room where Molly poured them both a glass of lemonade. Jordyn took a sip, smiled politely, but put the glass down and pushed it further away from her. The lemonade was watered down and was missing a crucial ingredient. Sugar, perhaps. Or maybe lemons.

Molly stared over at Jordyn as if she had something she wanted to say, but when she didn't speak, it was Jordyn who broke the silence.

"Is there a reason you asked me here today?" She didn't mean to sound impolite, but she believed in taking a direct approach. Frida was watching Aubrey again, and even if Jordyn didn't feel as close to her daughter as she wished she could, she also didn't like the idea of another woman raising her child. And if she was going to enjoy a day amongst adults, she wasn't sure if Molly was the person she'd want to spend it with.

Molly smiled. "I thought maybe we could get to know each other better. I've seen you around town. I know we were sort of friends in high school..." She trailed off.

Her reason felt weak and Jordyn suspected there was more to the visit. "That sounds nice," she said hesitantly. "Well, what have you been up to lately?"

A blush crept across Molly's cheeks, then she quickly composed herself. "You know, a little this. A little of that. I took on extra shifts at the diner recently. Tips are good. Especially on Friday nights."

Jordyn considered this. Molly had stayed thin. She had a pretty face. And with that charming accent, she probably made more on tips than she did with her regular paycheck. She kept these thoughts to herself and instead said, "I'll have to come in sometime. It's been a while since I've eaten there."

Molly smirked. "Doesn't seem like your kind of place."

Jordyn frowned involuntarily. The old her had loved that diner. She and Brody had gone to it many times. Greasy food. Fun-loving crowd. Loud music blaring from the jukebox. She felt homesick at the memory of Brody holding her hand across the booth and singing along under his breath whenever his favorite song came on.

Throat constricting with emotion, she asked, "May I use your bathroom?" The last thing she wanted to do was break down and cry on this woman's tattered sofa.

"Of course. It may not be at its best," she warned. "I don't have a housekeeper."

Jordyn didn't miss the hint of bitterness in her tone but when she didn't respond to it, Molly said, "It's just down the hall."

She followed the orange, shag carpeting until she reached the end of the hallway. To her left was the master bedroom. The door was partly ajar, allowing her to see inside. Faded, floral comforter. Mismatched pictures above an outdated four-poster bed of heavily scarred wood. Everything inside looked like it was purchased from a thrift store. Probably was. To the right of the master was a small bathroom. Jordyn slipped inside, then closed and locked the door behind her.

Once she was alone, a full-on panic attack came on. Her breathing became erratic and her chest felt tight. *Breathe in and out, in and out* she reminded herself as she bent forward and put her head between her knees. Nothing felt right. Nothing. She pressed her hand over her mouth to muffle the cries that escaped her lips. She was trapped in a reality she hated. A reality that she'd once been so sure she wanted. Her own personal hell she'd once imagined would be heaven.

It took her a few moments to compose herself. She stood up tall and crossed to the sink to splash cold water on her face. The modest vanity was covered with inexpensive makeup and off-brand face lotions. Jordyn made a face at the used razor sitting on the counter and did her best not to knock any of the clutter into the sink. The medicine cabinet was ajar. It was also untidy. There were pill bottles, toothpaste, a trial-size bottle of mouthwash. And there, on the bottom shelf, was a bottle of *Vanilla Ecstasy* perfume. She remembered Kane coming home with the smell of vanilla on his clothes and in that instant, she knew why Molly had invited her over.

Trying to find order in a world quickly spinning out of control, Jordyn straightened the medicine cabinet. She closed the cabinet door, dried her face with a clean towel from the cabinet under the sink, then folded the towel and placed it neatly atop the existing, crusty hand towel. She stared at her reflection a final time until she convinced herself she'd removed all traces of shock and devastation. Then she plastered a smile on her face and returned to the living room where Molly was waiting.

"So, the diner," Jordyn said lightly. "Lots of late nights, huh?"

Molly blushed again. "Well, lots of long days. Mostly late Friday nights." She appeared to be choosing her words carefully.

"Late nights must be going around."

"What do you mean?" Molly sat up straighter and cleared her throat uncomfortably.

"I mean Kane's been having quite a few late nights himself." She raised an eyebrow and gave Molly a pointed stare, but the smile never left Jordyn's face.

"Is there something you want to ask me?" This time Molly's southern accent seemed exaggerated. As if she thought it would make her sound more innocent.

Tight smile. Pointed stare. Jordyn said, "No. Nothing I need to *ask*. Was there something you wanted to *tell* me?"

Molly's lower lip quivered and her big eyes welled with tears. "I'm not a bad person, you know."

Jordyn's cold, hard stare didn't waiver. She wasn't about to let Molly off the hook.

"I never meant for anything to happen. He told me you two weren't in love anymore."

"Perhaps. Yet..." Jordyn raised her ring finger and tapped her wedding ring with her thumb. "Still married." She was remarkably calm. A strange feeling engulfed her. She couldn't decipher what it was. Relief, perhaps. Could that really be it?

"Jordyn, I'm so sorry..."

"Save it. Why did you ask me here today? Were you hoping to get a big reaction from me? Hoping you'd drop the bomb of your affair and I'd what, leave Kane and he'd come running to you?"

Hot tears streaked down Molly's cheeks. "I wanted to get to know you better," she wailed. "I guess I wanted you to be this cruel, awful person so I could feel better."

"And? Did this help?" Calm. Jordyn remained ever so calm.

"No," Molly whispered, her head hung low.

"No, I don't imagine it did." She stood to go. She slung her purse over her shoulder, crossed to the door, then turned to face Molly. "You know, men willing to have an affair rarely leave their spouses for their mistress."

Molly nodded, knowingly.

"And even if they do," Jordyn said, "the pattern continues."

Molly nodded again, no longer able to make eye contact.

"Now, I'm no fool. But I also need time to sort things out. If you have any decency. If you care about what you'd do to a family. What you'd do to Aubrey. I ask that you stay away while I do that."

"I can't promise that," Molly said, chin jutting upward. She sounded stronger. More indignant.

"And I can't promise I won't punch that pretty face of yours if I catch you with him." Jordyn's smile was sickeningly sweet. "Thank you for the lemonade. I'll show myself out."

Despite her calm demeanor as she walked out Molly's door, Jordyn was a wreck by the time her car pulled out of the drive. She was devastated. But surprisingly, not for the life she'd thought she had with Kane. Instead, she grieved for the life she once had with Brody.

Bitter tears streaked down her face as her emotions crashed in on her all at once. She sucked in her breath to recover, trying to control her pain as she wished for the thousandth time that she could call Hailie. Her mind drifted to Brody, as it often did, and how his face lit up each time his two older brothers came into town. As an only child, Jordyn mostly considered herself lucky to have had so much of her parents' love and affection to herself. She'd been spoiled. But it was in moments like these that she wished she had a sibling to lean on.

She took the long way home. She needed to face Kane and reveal all she knew. But she didn't feel any urgency to do so at that very moment. She travelled into town instead. She circled the place where *Homespun Goodness* should be, then the police station, before begrudgingly making her way to the grand house that she was now convinced more than ever could never truly be a home.

Chapter Twenty-Seven

Brody attended church as he did every Sunday morning. He starched and ironed his one dress shirt and headed out early to get his favorite seat. Back row, far outside corner. It allowed him the best view of the entire congregation and gave him the option of a quick getaway if he got a call. Outsiders would call him a devoted Christian. But his reasons for attending service so faithfully had little to do with his devotion to church. Rather, it was the one day a week he was almost guaranteed to catch a glimpse of Jordyn. Of course it pained him to see her walk through those double doors on the arm of Kane Masters. But even that fact couldn't take away the exhilarating feelings that coursed through his veins every time he saw her.

When she walked in that morning, Brody smiled to himself when he realized she was alone. No sign of Kane or Aubrey, which he thought was unusual. She'd missed church altogether the previous Sunday, which was even more unusual. His joy turned to worry. He hoped everything was okay.

Jordyn walked down the center aisle. She cast a glance in his direction, smiled shyly, then sat one row in front of him. More towards the middle, which gave him a perfect view of her. Usually dressed to the nines for church, Brody was surprised to see her in a pair of jeans and a button up flannel shirt. Her hair was pulled back in a loose ponytail and she wore minimal makeup. With the sun shining through the church windows, she looked like an angel.

Brody couldn't recall when she'd ever looked more beautiful. He shifted uncomfortably in his seat. The choir began to sing and he reminded himself, as he did every Sunday, that Jordyn was a married woman. The preacher chose that morning of all mornings to preach about forbidden fruit and Brody sat back in the pew, finding humor in the irony.

During the service he noticed Jordyn glancing back at him. Each time she did, he glanced away, realizing he'd been caught staring. But when the service was nearing an end, he caught her gaze and held it. Her stare seemed to indicate she needed to talk to him.

He planned to track her down after the service, but he didn't have to. By the time he reached the bottom step, she'd caught up to him.

"Brody, hi," she said, a bit out of breath. Her cheeks were flushed pink by the cold. And perhaps for him.

"Good morning," he said in his most professional tone. "You're here alone today, I see. Everything okay at home?"

"Always playing the protective cop," she said.

He thought he caught a hint of bitterness in her tone but he let it slide. When he didn't respond to her comment, she said, "Kane had some paperwork to catch up on at home and Aubrey said she wanted to sleep in, so..."

He nodded.

She'd lied of course. Truth was, she'd planned to confront Kane about his infidelity but he was blind drunk by the time he got home. Frida offered to stay the night to help with Aubrey and Jordyn had taken her up on it.

"I was going to head over to the diner to grab something to eat," Jordyn said. She hesitated, nibbling on her bottom lip. "Did you, um, want to join me?"

"You eat at that greasy old diner?" he asked, surprised.

Another person who thought she acted too good to eat there. "What do you mean? I love that place." In another life, that diner had been the location of her and Brody's first date. It was a place they'd frequented when neither were in the mood to cook. It stung that he had no recollection, though it was through no fault of his own.

He stroked his chin, looking doubtful. "You've always struck me as a linen tablecloths and candlelight dinner sort of woman."

She made a face. "Nah, those types of places don't have karaoke on Friday nights."

Brody grinned. "Now I know you're messing with me. I've been to karaoke night at the diner tons of times. I'm fairly certain I've never seen you there."

"Wait. *You* frequent karaoke night?" Despite their regular trips to the diner in their past life, Jordyn had never seen Brody take an interest in singing karaoke.

He crossed his arms in front of his chest and smiled broadly. "I'm usually more of a curious spectator."

Jordyn nodded. That seemed more like him.

"Other times I've been called there in the line of duty."

Eyebrow raised, she asked, "They arrest people around these parts for singing off key?"

He chuckled. "Believe it or not, people get a little rowdy on Friday nights at the old greasy spoon."

Jordyn laughed, then her expression became more serious. She almost lost her nerve, but she swallowed her pride and pressed forward. "So, how is it at lunchtime?"

"Crowded." His tone indicated he thought the diner was a bad idea.

She narrowed her eyes as she mulled over his hesitation. Trying to figure him out, she asked, "You worried someone might see us?"

"Aren't you?"

She shrugged her slender shoulders. "Two old friends having lunch. Seems harmless. What's to worry about?"

His eyes flashed with mischief and his mouth curved into an amused smile. When Jordyn shivered, he instinctively reached over and buttoned the top button of her coat. "Is that what we are? Two old friends."

"More or less." She shrugged again, outwardly looking both sure of herself and completely at ease. But inside her stomach was a flutter of nerves. Even though she'd probably die of exposure, she wanted to unbutton every button of her coat so she could have the pleasure of him buttoning it back up again.

"Tell you what," Brody said. "Let's do lunch. But how about back at the precinct?"

"Am I under arrest? Being questioned in a crime?"

His eyes locked with hers. "Have you something to confess?"

She grinned but didn't answer. She was thinking about all those nights he took her in his arms. How it felt to have his warm, hungry lips on hers. She swam in guilt that each time she kissed Kane, it was Brody's face she saw. Brody whom she longed to touch and to be touched by in return. If the sheriff could read her thoughts, he'd see she had a shocking amount to confess.

"I'll order in some sandwiches. My office is quiet. More private." He stared over at her and his big brown eyes flickered with mischief. "Perfect conditions for two old friends to catch up."

"Alright, I'm game. You order the sandwiches and I'll meet you there in say, thirty minutes?"

On the drive to the police station, Brody realized he had no earthly idea where his assistant, Cora, bought the sandwiches he loved so much.

-168-

Some detective skills he had. He never paid attention to the logo on the sandwich wrapping, or the paper bag it came in. He called Cora to ask her.

"I can just order for you and swing it by the station."

"But it's your day off."

"Nonsense. What else am I going to do?" she said. Then before Brody could refuse her offer, she asked, "Your usual?"

When Brody told her *yes*, but that he'd need two, and two sweet teas to go with them, he heard her pause. He could tell she was resisting the urge to ask who the second sandwich was for and he was grateful she refrained from doing so. He supposed she'd find out soon enough. With Jordyn's curve-hugging jeans and tall boots it was unlikely she would blend in at the station. She wouldn't blend in anywhere.

"Anything else?" his assistant interrupted his errant thoughts.

"Err, that will do it. I'll be at the station in…say…twenty minutes."

Once he reached his office and his assistant dropped off the sandwiches, he started to worry Jordyn would change her mind. She'd been acting so different lately. Unpredictable. Almost irrational. It kept him on edge. He loved every minute of it.

He didn't have to wonder for long. She swept into his office like a burst of fresh air.

"Those sandwiches smell amazing," she said.

"So do you." The words were out of his mouth before he had time to think about them. They shocked his ears, but he refused to regret saying them.

"Thank you," she said, smiling sweetly and taking the compliment in stride. She was anything but offended. She knew he would love the way she smelled. She was wearing *Ardor*, his favorite perfume. It was a fragrance they'd discovered together at *Rosewater Boutique* downtown while they'd been out Christmas shopping a few years earlier. Jordyn disliked the designer perfumes that lined the vanity in her new home. But she loved *Ardor's* aroma of spicy and sweet. And the decent price tag that came with it.

On a whim, she'd dropped into the little boutique on her way to the police station. She knew the shop would still carry it. She'd been purchasing it there for years. Still, she breathed a sigh of relief at seeing it perched on the shelf towards the back. She applied a subtle amount to her neck and wrists before sauntering into the station to see Brody for their *harmless* lunch between *two old friends*.

Brody took a seat behind his desk and Jordyn sat across from him. He removed his baseball cap and tossed it on the shelf behind him. His floppy hair revealed he needed a haircut, but Jordyn thought it made him look even more charming. And sexy. Her heart fluttered as she wondered how she'd ever thought she could live without him.

By this time she was starving and she unwrapped the packaging and dug hungrily into her sandwich. "Oh my gosh," she said with a mouthful of food. "Mmm...this is so good."

Brody grinned, then delved into his own sandwich. He closed his eyes in appreciation. But it wasn't the sandwich he was savoring. It was watching Jordyn's pretty mouth as she ate. Smelling her perfume linger in the air. And wishing for the hundredth time that day they were more than just the old friends she claimed they were.

When Jordyn looked up from her food to ask a question, Brody started to chuckle.

"What's so funny?"

"Um, you have a bit of mayo on your lip. Here, let me." Without thinking, he reached across the desk to touch her face. Unable to stop himself, he stroked her soft cheek. His brow furrowed as he reminded himself, she wasn't his. He pressed his thumb to her lips. Instinctively Jordyn's lips parted and she sucked on the tip of his thumb. His eyes widened in surprise and arousal at her provocation.

"It's all gone," he said, scooting backwards in his chair to put some distance between them.

"It's all… Oh," Jordyn said, the mayo already forgotten. "Well, thank you." She flushed, suddenly unsure of herself.

Silence filled the small room. Brody's thoughts were in turmoil as he searched for the right thing to say. "Do you love him?" he finally blurted out.

Jordyn's eyes widened in surprise. Then she did something unexpected. She smiled. "Would it change things if I didn't?"

Brody shifted uncomfortably in his chair but didn't respond.

She shook her head, still laughing. "We're a mess, you and I."

Grunting in acknowledgement, he said, "Yep. We make quite a pair." His eyes locked with hers. A mutual understanding that there was more meaning in his words than he could convey. At that moment they both knew exactly how they felt about each other, but also understood neither could act on their deeply rooted feelings.

"Well, I should go," Jordyn finally said, already wondering how she'd explain her absence to Kane. She crumpled up the empty sandwich wrappings, took a final swig of her tea, then tossed both into the trash. As she stood to her feet, she said, "Brody, this has been…lovely."

"Always a pleasure," he told her.

She left him alone to sort out his thoughts and jumbled feelings. Her scent lingered long after she'd gone.

Chapter Twenty-Eight

Throughout the years she was in a relationship with Brody, Jordyn received several late-night phone calls from him. Check-ins to let her know he was working late. Or that he was finally on the way home. Sometimes he'd call because he was processing one of the locals to spend the night in the drunk tank. But now that she was married to Kane, late-night phone calls from Brody weren't anything she'd come to expect. Which is why she was so surprised when he called her after two a.m. on a Tuesday morning.

"Is everything okay?" she asked, shooting straight up in bed and fumbling for the light switch next to the nightstand.

"Yes, yes, everything's fine," Brody said soothingly.

"What time is it?" She could see the clock on the nightstand and knew dang well what time it was. But given the shockingly early hour, her question was more sarcastic in nature.

"It's about 2:15 in the morning." He paused. "Just after closing time."

"I see," Jordyn said. "What's Kane done?"

"Nothing, really. He just got a bit rowdy at *JB's Bar*. Owner kicked him out and called us."

"Good for JB." Then she felt guilty about her unexpected outburst. After her meeting with Molly, she'd planned to have it out with Kane, but the bastard hadn't bothered to come home that night and after that, she didn't much see the point. She'd toyed with the idea of having her own affair. Figured she could justify it to herself. But she knew Brody would never agree to it. What with his morals and chivalry and all.

Brody grinned from the other end of the line. Jordyn's words were his sentiments exactly.

"So, you need me to pick him up then?" As much as she'd like to see Brody, she dreaded the idea of waking up Aubrey and heading out in the middle of the night.

"Nah," he said. "I thought we'd let him sleep it off. Just wanted to let you know where he was so you didn't worry."

This time it was Jordyn's turn to smile. She should be furious with Kane. Probably was if she stopped to think about it. But at that moment all she could think about was how thoughtful it was for Brody to call her so she didn't worry.

"Jordyn, you there?"

"Yes, sorry. I'm here."

"We'll get him back to his truck in the morning. Should have him back to you by breakfast time."

She wanted to mouth off that Brody was welcome to keep Kane for as long as he pleased. She also thought about insisting that if Kane was going to be home by breakfast, he may just need to come home earlier to prepare it. But she bit her tongue and simply said, "Thank you, Brody. I really appreciate it."

"My pleasure."

Jordyn laughed.

"Sorry, that came out wrong." He cleared his throat. "I just meant, it's no trouble."

"Yeah, it is," she said matter-of-factly, "but nonetheless, I appreciate you saying it's not."

Brody closed his eyes, felt a squeeze around his heart as he pictured Jordyn's sleepy face. He blinked to erase the pleasant image from his mind.

"Goodnight, Jordyn." He needed to end their conversation before he got too comfortable and started telling her how he really felt. About Kane. About her.

Closing her eyes and pretending he was lying next to her, she whispered back, "Goodnight, Brody."

They both waited on the line for a few, silent moments before Brody said, "Go back to sleep Jordyn."

She grinned to herself before disconnecting the call.

As much as Jordyn appreciated Frida's cooking, and her company, some days it was a relief to have the kitchen to herself. So when Frida called in sick that morning, she took full advantage of her alone time. She padded around the kitchen in her pajamas, making breakfast and listening to Christmas music that was piped into all the rooms in the house. Despite the chaos, Aubrey slept through it all. Jordyn fried bacon, eggs, and potatoes and made freshly squeezed orange juice. All the while she pondered if Kane would call before coming home. And if he even knew the sheriff had called her so she wouldn't worry.

She smiled again, thinking about Brody. Having breakfast together used to be one of their favorite things. They'd curl up on the sofa with their plates of food and enjoy an intimate morning of companionable silence, unspoiled by the morning news or other unwanted distractions. A crackling fire and the occasional song of a Gray Jay were their only disruptions.

Pushing him out of her mind, she returned her focus to the avocado she was slicing up for her toast. Frida had a knack for picking out perfectly ripe avocadoes. But not bananas, Jordyn thought, smiling to herself as she eyed the enormous fruit bowl on the kitchen counter. A small bushel of brown bananas sat perched on top, surrounded by fresh apples and oranges. Jordyn plucked the bananas from the bowl and put them in the freezer. Later she'd make the walnut and banana bread Brody loved so much. She didn't bother to remind herself she'd probably never get to share the bread with him again. The thought was too painful.

She heard a rustling on the front porch, followed by an alert on her phone, letting her know someone was outside. She picked up her phone and glanced at the front stoop camera feed. As she suspected, it was Kane. She set her phone back on the counter and went back to cooking breakfast. She wouldn't fight with him, she decided. It wouldn't do any good. If Brody had pulled a stunt like that, they would have had quite the row, and then made up in the bedroom after scarfing down the breakfast they would have been shoveling down during the argument. They had hated arguing. Loved their food. Loved to make up even more. But Brody wouldn't have pulled a stunt like that. And therein was the difference.

Jordyn thought it odd she was choosing not to even discuss the topic. How quickly she had changed. She wondered how long it had taken the other version of herself to wear down. How many months or years into marrying Kane had she given up self and given in to the way things were.

She heard the front door open, then close softly. The lack of slamming told her Kane's mood was either pleasant or contrite. That much was a comfort, at least.

When Kane walked into the kitchen, she said, "Good morning," with the sunniest disposition she could muster. Hair disheveled and shirt half untucked, he flashed her a crooked grin. There was a time his mischievous smile and large dimples would have melted her heart. She smiled back at him, pretending they still did.

"What's for breakfast?" he asked. "Smells good in here."

"Oh, I'm sorry," she said with a feigned apology. "I wasn't sure what time you'd be home, so I only made enough for me."

His expression clouded and his eyes went dark.

"But I could either give you this one or fix you a fresh plate," she amended, hating how once again she was giving in.

"That would be great," he told her. His good mood returned so she figured taking a few minutes to make him breakfast was a small sacrifice in exchange for keeping the peace.

"Aubrey still asleep?" he asked.

"You know Aubrey, she loves to sleep in late on the days she doesn't have school."

That was an assumption Jordyn hoped she knew to be true. Perhaps it wasn't the norm, but certainly had been for the few weeks she recalled of their lives together.

He laughed knowingly. "I'm going to grab a quick shower then I'll join you for breakfast."

"It'll be waiting for you," she said sweetly. Too sweetly. If he knew her at all, he'd know underneath that sugary smile was spit and vinegar.

"Did you worry about me?" he asked over the breakfast of eggs and potatoes she'd prepared for him while he was in the shower (and had purposely oversalted).

"Nope, they called from the jail to let me know you were being booked." She was careful not to mention Brody's name. Not only because Kane seemed testy whenever she mentioned the sheriff. But she was also worried what her expression might reveal.

Realizing she should at least show some emotion for the night Kane had spent in jail, she furrowed her brow and said, "Were you okay?"

"Sure. Just a couple pompous officers trying to throw their weight around. But they should know payback's not far off."

Jordyn bit her lip nervously. "What do you mean?" She reached across the table and took his hand in hers. "You won't do anything rash will you?" Then, fearing it sounded like her worry was for the officers and not for her husband (which was indeed the case), she said, "I'd hate to see you get in trouble."

His smile was dismissive and condescending. "Don't you worry your pretty little head about it."

She smiled back. But inside she was seething.

Changing the subject, he asked, "Now, does Frida know that you prepare eggs better than she does?"

Jordyn smiled to herself. Perhaps she hadn't added as much salt as she'd thought. "No, and you're not going to tell her," she said, pretending to scold him. "And once you finish those, I have a cobbler coming out of the oven."

She hoped Kane liked cobbler. She had no idea what he liked she realized. Besides platinum-haired, passive women, apparently.

Chapter Twenty-Nine

"**A**re you gonna have pancakes for breakfast Momma?" Aubrey's bright blue eyes shone with excitement. Breakfast was her favorite meal. She loved fruit. Syrup. Powdered sugar. All the sweets. A big breakfast was also the clever way Frida bribed her out of bed to go to school.

Jordyn glanced over and smiled at the plate of pancakes with melted chocolate chips shaped into smiley faces.

"Thanks Frida. You've made her day."

Frida smiled, embarrassed by the compliment, and continued to move about the kitchen. She poured a glass of orange juice and set it in front of Jordyn. "I also made pancakes without the faces," she offered.

"I'll take one of both, thank you."

Frida plated the pancakes and poured syrup over them. It was the precise amount of syrup Jordyn liked and at first, she was amazed. Then she realized her housekeeper had likely been doing this for her for years. She wondered how she'd treated Frida in the past. When she'd first awoken in her *new life*, the housekeeper hadn't seemed overly friendly, so Jordyn reckoned she had kept things purely professional and had failed to make friends with a woman who could have been her biggest ally. Jordyn didn't like the person she was discovering she was in this current reality. She was sort of a snob.

"Where's Daddy, Momma?"

Aubrey's sweet voice interrupted her thoughts. At the innocent question, Jordyn swallowed the lump in her throat. She didn't know what to tell the little girl who worshipped her daddy so much. She hesitated, but Frida came to the rescue.

"He must still be sleeping, angel." She gave Jordyn a knowing look. "How about after breakfast I take you to the toy store before you have to go to preschool? Maybe you can show me the toys you asked Santa for."

"Thank you," Jordyn mouthed. The truth was Kane hadn't come home last night and she didn't have any idea how to explain that to Aubrey. She supposed she could have told her he'd left early to work, but she also wasn't certain if she could lie so blatantly to her daughter. The poor little girl didn't need two dishonest parents.

Last night wasn't the first time Kane hadn't come home. And hadn't bothered to call. From what Jordyn was starting to piece together, it was a regular thing for him. She thought of her other life. Thought of Molly. And that's when she realized this was likely the life Molly had lived. Tied down to a selfish jerk who couldn't be faithful if his entire fortune depended upon it. And Jordyn had been so sure she'd wanted to be with him. So sure that, somehow, her desires had become a reality. And it turned out she got far more than she'd bargained for.

It wasn't until Aubrey was dressed to head off to preschool with Frida, and she'd kissed her goodbye, that Jordyn finally broke down and had a good cry. But she didn't cry out of any love for Kane. She cried for everything she'd lost in her prior life. She cried for the love she had with Brody. Baby or no baby—what she and Brody had shared had been real. Now she had a daughter she didn't recall giving birth to and a shell of a marriage she'd happily give away.

After she'd collected herself, she took a steaming shower and changed into jeans and a button-up flannel shirt. Then she went to the reading room to settle in with a book. It used to be easy for her to get lost in a book, but these days, when it seemed all she did was read, she found herself easily distracted. And bored. She needed someone to talk to. Human contact. Adult interaction.

"Maybe I should get a dog," she spoke aloud to herself. In another life, it was the type of thing she would have discussed with Hailie. Had discussed with Hailie, actually. But since she had no idea where in the universe Hailie was, and apparently this universe didn't come with any friends at all, she was her only audience.

"Mr. Masters is allergic to dogs," she heard Mr. Davis speak up behind her.

She jumped and spun around. "Oh, I'm sorry Mr. Davis, I didn't hear you come in." She cleared her throat, uncomfortable. He probably thought she was going crazy, talking to herself like that. And he was probably correct.

He offered her a kind smile as he began to load wood into the fireplace. "They do have hypoallergenic dogs," he said. "My aunt's typically allergic, but she was able to find one of those designer dogs. You know they sort of look like rats, and yelp at every car horn, but hey, at least nobody's sneezing."

Jordyn flashed him a grin. "I was just thinking out loud. I guess I was lonely," she admitted, not sure why she was sharing so much.

Mr. Davis gave her a knowing nod. "Hairless cats are also an option," he quipped.

Jordyn laughed. For the first time in days. Once she started, she couldn't stop. Perhaps it was because it had been so long since she'd felt so lighthearted. As tears of laughter rolled down her cheeks, she clutched her sides. "Oh, thank you Mr. Davis, I needed that."

"It's what I'm here for," he said dryly, but he had a twinkle in his eyes. Then he wandered off to perform his duties, leaving Jordyn in a good mood with a brighter outlook than she'd had moments prior.

Jordyn checked her watch. She still had a couple hours until Frida picked up Aubrey from preschool. She could run into town and be back in time to enjoy an afternoon snack with her daughter. It was a new tradition she was trying to implement and one of the highlights of her day.

On her way out, she glanced at her reflection in the hallway mirror. Despite the quick application of mascara, her eyes looked hollowed. Sad. She tucked in her flannel shirt, then cocked her head to the side. She thought of changing into something sexier, but then figured it would look like she was trying too hard. She was going to see the sheriff on official business, she reminded herself. Nothing more.

Chapter Thirty

"Is everything okay?" Brody asked, surprised by Jordyn's presence in his office. Pleasantly surprised. Something about her made him feel giddy—like he was back in high school and on his first date. She swept into the room wearing a baggie flannel shirt tucked into faded jeans and looking more beautiful than any runway model.

"Yes, everything's fine," she said without a trace of unease. "Totally fine." Her green eyes shone bright and her cheeks were pink from the outside cold.

He breathed a sigh of relief. He worried about her. As sheriff, it was his job to worry about the safety and well-being of people in his town. But with Jordyn, it went deeper than that. It was a truth he'd never admit aloud.

"How are things with you?" she asked.

He could tell she was genuinely interested and it stirred him. "Everything's great. You know how it gets around the holidays. More crowds. Some trouble with a few rowdy tourists. But nothing I can't handle." He didn't mention the increase in crime. He didn't want to worry her.

She nodded but didn't say anything further. She was searching for a good intro to ask him for a favor.

Turned out she didn't have to come up with one.

"But you didn't come here to ask how I was doing, did you?" he said with a knowing grin.

"You're right," she admitted. "I was hoping you could do something for me."

His brown eyes locked with hers. "Name it." His tone held no hesitation.

Jordyn gazed back at him, realizing he meant it. His look suggested she could ask for anything at that moment. Recognizing this made her feel guilty since she'd need to be evasive with her request. Then she remembered the auction she'd need to ask him about as well. As awkward as that request might be, at least she could be transparent.

"So, the town's having an auction at the next fundraiser."

"So I've heard," Brody said, still grinning.

"Of course you've heard," Jordyn said, rolling her eyes.

"Well, it's hard not to notice when my name is on the flyer." He pointed to the corkboard above his desk. The flyer proudly presented Brody as one of the men to be auctioned off.

Jordyn was mortified. "I guess Latrisha didn't waste any time putting that together. I'm so sorry, Brody. I was supposed to ask if you'd be willing to participate. I didn't realize the committee would move forward with the flyers so quickly."

He shrugged. "Forget about it. Happy to do it."

Jordyn's heart melted. Brody made things easy. It was a breath of fresh air after putting up with Kane. "I know that's not true, but I appreciate your willingness."

He studied her. "And your other request?"

"Pardon?"

"I know that's not the only reason you came here today." His eyes twinkled with humor.

She hesitated, biting her bottom lip. "I have a name I was hoping you could run down," she confessed sheepishly.

Brody cocked his head to the side. His beautiful, brown eyes narrowed with curiosity. "Are you trying to be your own detective?" he teased.

She laughed nervously. "No. Nothing as aspirational as that. It's just an old acquaintance I'd like to get back in touch with." She failed to look him in the eye as she only revealed half-truths.

Brody knew she wasn't being transparent about her reasons, but he also knew he'd never deny her anything. Especially such a simple request. "I'll see what I can do," he said. He was noncommittal. Not because he didn't plan to look into it for her. Rather, if it turned out whatever he was looking into would reveal information that would cause her pain, like perhaps an affair, he had plausible deniability.

"Thank you, Brody," Jordyn told him, making a mental note about his hesitation. Perhaps she'd misread his earlier enthusiasm. "I really appreciate it." She reached out her hand to shake his.

When he took her hand in his, it felt soft and warm. He tried to ignore the way her touch sent shockwaves through his system. Kane didn't deserve a woman like her. And unfortunately, proving it to her would serve only to hurt her.

"So, how should I reach you?" he asked. His eyes burned into hers.

"Pardon?" She felt flushed at his touch.

"If I find information... Literally the reason you came in here," he said, grinning.

"Right. Sorry." She took a breath. "Sorry, I have been so distracted these days."

He studied her again. "You sure everything's okay?" A strand of her hair had escaped her ponytail and he resisted the urge to reach up and tuck it behind her ear.

Her eyes misted as she considered his question. She didn't need him to protect her, but she adored the fact that he wanted to. She blew out a slow breath, then said, "Sometimes, I just think…" But she stopped, dismissing her own thoughts with a wave of her hand. "Nope, nope, I am not going to bother you with this. Sorry Brody. I promise you everything is fine." She smiled up at him through the tears in her eyes.

Then she said, "You can call me."

"Pardon?"

"If you find out any information." This time it was her turn to remind him about what they'd been discussing.

He chuckled. "Oh, right. That." He paused. "Kane won't mind?"

"Kane's never around to care," she said bitterly. Then her cheeks turned pink and she bit her lip. "Apologies, that was a bit of an overreaction. What I meant to say was, he won't mind."

He didn't press her further. "Great, I'll call you then. If I'm able to find anything."

"Great," she said, turning to go.

As she walked away, Brody called after her. "Jordyn."

"Yes?" Her heart fluttered that he seemed to want her to stay. She turned to face him.

"Do you have that name?"

She blushed three shades of red, pulled a slip of paper out of her pocket and handed it to him, then made a quick exit before she could humiliate herself further. Or before she could beg Brody to take her back no matter what alternate reality they'd be living out the rest of their lives in.

Brody was exhausted by the time he walked through the front door of his empty house. He trudged to the fridge, grabbed the milk, and drank straight out of the carton. It was a disgusting habit his mother had never allowed while he was growing up, but now there wasn't anyone around to stop him. He should give his mother a call, he realized. It had been about a week since he'd spoken to her. They were close, but sometimes his job distracted him from reaching out as often as he'd like. That, and sometimes he couldn't face hearing his mother's disappointment when he admitted he still wasn't dating anyone special. He went on dates, sure. Mostly to appease his well-meaning friends and family who tried to set him up with any single female under thirty-five. But no one could hold a candle to Jordyn. And to pretend anyone could seemed like a waste of time. His and theirs.

He returned the milk to the fridge and took out cold chicken and a beer instead. He settled into his recliner and switched on the television, flipping mindlessly through the channels. His friend Paul had offered to come over and watch Christmas Vacation with him—an annual tradition—but Brody had had a rough day trying to push Jordyn out of his every thought and he didn't want his foul mood to rub off on anyone else. He'd made an excuse that he was working late. Now the lie was just another in a string of recent regrets.

Alone in his misery, his thoughts strayed once again to Jordyn. The woman who had never been his but somehow felt like the one who got away. He felt obliged to protect her. The need went beyond his job as sheriff. It felt...primal. Almost carnal.

Chapter Thirty-One

The evening of the auction arrived. Brody took the stage because that's what Jordyn had asked him to do. He had a confident air. Wide, crooked grin. Tall, ramrod posture. Only Jordyn recognized the apprehension in his gaze. The look of trepidation that he masked behind his beautiful, sparkling smile.

"We'll start the bidding at fifty dollars," the auctioneer announced.

"Fifty-five dollars," one of the town singles announced. Jordyn seethed silently behind her booth of baked goods and second-hand clothing.

"Seventy-five dollars," the recently widowed Beatrice Harper chimed in. She waved her checkbook in the air as if the gesture somehow made her bid more credible.

Jordyn wanted to bid in the thousands and end the whole affair but she figured that wouldn't go over well with the town folks—or with Kane, who was next on the auction block.

Please come back to me Brody and I'll pay any price, she thought to herself. "C'mon ladies, you can do better than that," she shouted instead for the sake of a successful fundraiser.

"Two hundred dollars," a confident voice in the back of the crowd spoke up.

The auctioneer used his hand as a shield against the harsh, fluorescent lighting of the grange hall as he strained to see the mysterious bidder in the back of the crowd. "Two hundred dollars. Bid goes to…" He trailed off, still not clear who had made the bid.

"Molly Hauser," Molly piped up from the back of the room.

Brody's eyes flashed to Jordyn's. His expression wasn't something she could quite register but she smiled and gave him a thumbs up. When she did, his sensuous lips curved into a smile and he seemed to relax.

It was Kane who, Jordyn observed, was not smiling. He wasn't bothering to mask the heavy scowl on his face. Jordyn followed his gaze and realized his dark look was pointed in Molly's direction. She wanted to pretend her husband's soured mood was due to his disdain for the sheriff. After all, if Brody's bid exceeded his, that would be an embarrassment. A blow to his large, but rather fragile ego. But she knew there was more to it than that. She'd recognize that look anywhere. Kane was furiously jealous that Molly bid on Brody instead of him—and he wasn't even trying to hide it.

"And the winning bid goes to Molly Hauser," the auctioneer announced, slamming down his gavel before moving onto the next participant.

"Next up we have none other than thee Kane Masters. While he might not be single, I'm told he is good with tools and loves to help the ladies with anything they might need."

Jordyn rolled her eyes. Kane strolled confidently to the stage and took his place beside the auctioneer. When he tipped his hat, Jordyn thought she could hear the ladies swoon.

"We'll start the bidding at fifty dollars," the auctioneer said once again.

"A thousand dollars," Jordyn piped up. She wasn't sure what had come over her, but she'd be damned if she was about to allow one of these locals to have Kane to themselves when she was lucky to catch a dinner alone with him. But more than that, it was likely a kneejerk reaction to Molly getting to spend precious hours with Brody.

"Sold! Mr. Masters to Mrs. Masters for one thousand dollars," the auctioneer announced triumphantly.

There was a playful chorus of groans from the crowd. And a few dagger glares from the single ladies. Namely Molly Hauser, who tried to hide the look when Jordyn caught her eye. Molly covered her glare with a wide, ruby red smile, then made her way over to Brody so she could collect her *prize*. Jordyn's eyes flickered to Brody's, then to the floor. She blushed, trying to extinguish her shameful, longing thoughts. She'd been wondering if Molly would be willing to make a trade.

Kane was all smiles as he and Jordyn walked hand-in-hand out of the grange hall. But his smile turned to a scowl once they were alone.

"Why'd you convince me to do the auction if you were just going to swoop in before anyone else had a chance to bid?"

She couldn't believe he was angry. She figured he'd be flattered.

"I just wanted to make sure the auction was successful," she lied. "And I thought it might be nice for us to have a quiet evening to ourselves."

Kane grunted. "I may have some important business to tend to."

"Don't you think Molly's going to be busy with Brody?" she blurted out, no longer bothering to mask her irritation. Or her suspicions.

Kane didn't answer her. They drove home in silence. After Frida left, and Aubrey was tucked quietly into bed, Jordyn retired to her bedroom. Without a word, Kane grabbed his keys and left again.

Chapter Thirty-Two

Sheriff Brody stood back and studied the board. His eyes narrowed as he focused on every pinpoint that represented a piece of the puzzle. He skimmed his index finger across the red thread blazing a visual trail between each important datapoint.

FBI agent Clem McDaniels stood next to him. Used to electronic boards and other state-of-the-art technology, Clem found it fascinating the local authorities still used such rudimentary tools to solve major cases. But also impressed that Brody had managed to get so far in the case before bringing in outside help. The local sheriff was smart. His detective skills were advanced for such a small-town cop. DEA agent Marx Whitley had also been impressed with Brody's skills. Curious, he'd pulled a background on Brody, which he'd shared with Clem. The two men had been surprised to learn the sheriff had been a detective in San Francisco. And saddened to learn he'd lost his wife in such a tragic way.

"What are we missing?" Brody wondered aloud as he stared at the center of the board where a blank piece of paper was pinned instead of a suspect's picture.

Agent McDaniels wasn't sure if Brody was speaking to him but he replied just the same. "The suspect is going to be well-connected. Charming. He'd have to be both to smoothly run such a large operation and convince the right people to turn a blind eye."

"Nobody in my department is turning a blind eye," Brody defended.

Clem placed a reassuring hand on the sheriff's back. "Of course not." The agent suspected someone in the sheriff's department might be dirty, but now wasn't the time to bring it up. "I'm just saying, there's folks he would have had to pull into his operation. Neighbors. Shipping companies. Perhaps storefronts he'd need to use. That requires skill to convince a number of people to do things they perhaps wouldn't otherwise do."

Brody nodded. "Makes sense. What else?"

"He was likely already fairly successful. That would have given him the startup capital. Not to mention the clout. If that's the case, that means he's greedy. Or craves power. Or both." He paused. "And arrogant," he spat out, finishing the profile. "This bastard is arrogant enough to keep doing this right under our noses."

Brody nodded and stroked his chin. He could think of less than a half-dozen locals who fit that description. But at the top of the list, was Kane. From the beginning Brody suspected Kane was the financial backing behind the crime ring. He fit the profile to a tee. But Brody also feared his predisposed, strong dislike for the man might be hindering his judgement. Not to mention, no matter how deep he dug, Kane kept coming up clean. That's when Brody had decided to bring in outside reinforcements, but even the DEA and FBI had failed to divulge the ringmaster behind the recent rash of organized crime.

Brody took another step back from the board. An idea occurred to him. He realized he might have a way of digging up additional information on his prime suspect. He sighed with regret. It was a good plan, but it likely meant hurting someone who meant more to him than she'd ever know.

"Sheriff, we have Winnie in here for questioning," his deputy interrupted his thoughts.

He sighed. "Show her to interrogation room one." Then he called out, "And her name's Gwyneth. Treat her well and make sure she's comfortable."

Gwyneth waited in the interrogation room; her hands folded patiently in her lap. She was looking forward to seeing Sheriff Brody. He was a kind, honest man. She hoped he was faring well these days. She was rooting for him. After all, she wanted nothing but the best for him.

Chapter Thirty-Three

When Jordyn answered the phone that morning, the voice on the other end of the line wasn't who she expected.

"I have info on that name you asked me to run down," the familiar, gravelly voice told her.

She shot up in bed. Her heart pounded at hearing Brody's voice. She missed it. Missed being able to call him up at any time. Missed coming home to him every night and the way he always took an interest in her day. What she wouldn't give to curl up on the couch next to him and let him stroke her hair while they watched Jeopardy and sipped decaf coffee.

"Jordyn, you there?" the handsome sheriff asked in response to her silence.

"Yes, sorry." She pushed the hair out of her face with her hand and cleared her throat. "You were saying you found out something about Hailie Billings?"

He smiled at hearing her husky voice—evidence she hadn't yet spoken that morning.

"Yes, a little," he said. "I thought we could, I don't know...Maybe we could discuss it over breakfast?"

Jordyn mulled it over. Knowing how much Kane disliked the sheriff, would he see going to breakfast with Brody as a betrayal? Then again, she figured Kane was still betraying her in far worse ways. After all, he hadn't bothered to come home again last night. He claimed he needed to pull an all-nighter at the office. She wasn't even sure where or what *the office* was.

"Or I can just tell you now," he said in response to her hesitation.

"No, sorry, I was just…waking up, I guess. I could eat."

From the other end of the line, Brody muted the phone and sighed with relief. He was confused by his behavior. He'd always had a fondness for Jordyn. But she was a married woman. A woman whose husband was a powerful man. And Brody wasn't a homewrecker—no matter how much he disliked the husband.

"Brody?" This time it was Jordyn's turn to wonder about the silence on the phone.

"How about if I cook you breakfast at my place?"

Jordyn bit her lip. Although she was the baker out of the two, Brody had always held his own when it came to cooking. He could work magic with potatoes, eggs, and a seasoned skillet. She'd lost count of the early mornings he'd brought her breakfast in bed. They'd always made love afterwards. On rarer occasions, they'd stayed indoors all day and snuggled in front of the fireplace.

"I promise, no funny stuff," his voice interrupted her thoughts.

She laughed nervously. "Okay," she agreed, feeling brave.

"Thirty minutes?"

"It's wash-your-hair day. Can we make it forty-five?"

Brody chuckled. "I wouldn't want to stand between you and a good hair day. Take your time."

"Um, remind me where you live?"

"Seriously?" Brody felt a flicker of regret. She'd been to see him once. He remembered it like it was yesterday. The way she'd looked. The smell of her perfume. Her scent had lingered on his shirt long after she'd gone. Their brief embrace stayed with him. Haunted him. That day she'd been vulnerable and he, in a moment of weakness, had almost taken things too far. Based on Jordyn's hazy memory of where he lived, it was clear the interaction wasn't as memorable for her.

When Brody rattled off the address, Jordyn recognized it all too well. She felt homesick for the place they'd once shared. "You know, a good hair day is overrated. Let me throw on some clothes and make sure Frida can watch Aubrey. I'll be there in thirty." She hung up before she could talk herself out of it.

When Jordyn arrived outside of Brody's house, she paused on the front stoop. She missed her old place. While Brody had managed to put up some Christmas lights, gone were the personalized touches she'd added to the front porch. The hand-painted Welcome sign that Brody had teased her would draw unwanted guests. The terracotta flowerpots that led up the steps. In the warmer months, the pots would be stuffed full of geraniums and petunias. In the fall she'd swap the dying flowers out for boxwood plants. But despite the lack of outside décor, the house still had its rustic charm. It suited Brody. Suited her. More than Masters Manor ever could. She took a deep breath before knocking on the front door.

When Brody opened the door to her, she heard the familiar sound of the creaking hinges. The insignificant, yet unchanged detail from her former life brought her comfort. As did the smell of bacon wafting from the kitchen.

She inhaled in appreciation, then asked, "You going to invite me in?"

"Yes, sorry," he said, stepping aside to let her through.

She removed her coat, hat, and gloves, doing her best not to frown at the manicured nails she'd grown to hate. She offered a smile instead. "Smells amazing in here."

Grinning at the compliment, Brody led her to the kitchen where she put her belongings on the counter. It felt so familiar. He poured them each a glass of orange juice with a splash of champagne. Jordyn thought she could use more champagne but she kept the thought to herself. While she sipped her drink, Brody dished up two heaping plates of hash browns, eggs, sausage, and toast. Her stomach growled in response.

They didn't sit at the dining table, but instead took their seats on the living room couch in front of the fireplace. It felt cozy. Warm. Familiarly intimate.

"So, you have news for me on Hailie?" she asked through a mouthful of eggs.

"You don't waste any time, do you?" But he was already reaching into his shirt pocket for his notepad.

He flipped through a couple pages, cleared his throat, then said, "Hailie Billings. Moved to Sugarcreek three years ago. Lived here for just shy of three months, while she worked at the diner. Rumor has it she was a lousy waitress."

Jordyn laughed. Hailie was good with people but she could be a bit uncoordinated. Not to mention, forgetful. She could see how her friend wouldn't have made a very good waitress.

"Well, go on," she said once Brody paused.

"That's about it. She moved to Pittsburgh where she resides today. Works as a tour guide at some museum."

Jordyn's smile remained frozen on her face, but she felt a wave of sadness. Without a job at *Homespun Goodness*, Hailie hadn't found a reason to stay in Sugarcreek. She hadn't struck up a relationship with Tom Lacey from the hardware store. And worst of all, she hadn't become Jordyn's best friend. It seemed Jordyn didn't have any friends at all.

"Thank you for looking into her," she said, trying to mask the sadness in her eyes.

Brody nodded, noticing the way Jordyn fiddled with her earlobe. It seemed to be something she did when she was distressed. Almost like she was adjusting an earring, although she wasn't wearing any.

"Who was she to you?" he asked softly.

She shrugged. "Sort of a missed connection, I guess you could say."

He knew there was much more to it than that, but he let it go. They ate the remainder of the meal in silence. Brody admired the way, for such a petite woman, Jordyn could put away the food.

After polishing off the rest of their breakfast, he took their plates. Jordyn followed him into the kitchen where he topped off their glasses with more champagne. He held back the orange juice. Jordyn pressed the glass to her lips, wishing it were Brody's lips she was pressed up against instead. She drained her glass, sat it down on the countertop, and moved in closer to him.

He shifted his stance, uncomfortable.

"Do you ever think about us?" she asked through a fog of champagne and jumbled emotions.

He cleared his throat. "What do you mean?"

She could tell by his expression she had his full attention. "I think you know what I mean." Bravely, she moved in closer to him as she silently commanded the ground to steady beneath her feet. This time she did press her lips to his.

He pulled back, surprised. "Jordyn, we can't," he said. His expression was pained. "Believe me, I want to, but…"

"I know," she said with regret. "I'm married. And you're too honorable."

He grinned at her. He tucked a strand of her hair behind her ear as he waited for his breathing to return to normal. His fingertips grazed her skin, sending a pleasurable thrill through him. "Not really," he admitted. "But I'm trying hard to be."

She laughed, though her eyes glistened with tears. "Kane's cheating on me, you know. With Molly Hauser."

"I suspected," he admitted aloud.

She flushed. Of course he knew. He knew everything that happened in their little town. "And while I don't have any proof, I also suspect he's not a very honest businessman."

He nodded and his brown eyes softened. "I know that too."

"So why? Why should we hold ourselves to a higher standard?"

He stroked her cheek. The longing in his eyes was unmistakable. "Because we're better than him." As he said the words, he knew he was trying to convince himself more than he was her.

Jordyn's green eyes flashed with anger and passion. "Well, today I don't want to be. Today I just want…"

Brody didn't wait for her to finish. He pulled her into his arms and kissed her hard. His thoughts were jumbled and his conscience faltered as he swept his tongue inside her mouth.

Jordyn moaned softly as Brody's mouth claimed hers. She'd missed his warmth. His lips. Even more than she'd realized until that very moment. "Would it make sense if I told you I feel like I've kissed you a thousand times?" Her question was muffled by his kisses.

It didn't make sense, but Brody didn't need it to. He loved the way her words sounded when they rolled off her tongue. His heart hammered with desire as he nibbled greedily on her bottom lip. Her ripe lips tasted of passion and coconut.

Her perfume was just as he'd remembered. Warm and sweet with a touch of spice. He stroked her hair. It was soft despite the years of bleaching. He preferred the natural, chestnut color but either way she was beautiful. He loved her, he realized. Had loved her since the moment he'd come to this small town. It still pained him to recall their first meeting. How he'd been smitten, then crushed to realize she was already married. One look into her spirited green eyes and he'd been so convinced she was the one.

Jordyn's breath hitched as she felt Brody pull her closer. Her heart beat faster. She longed to be closer to him. Skin on skin. Her arms went around his waist as she melted against him, feeling the hardness of his arousal. A growl of desire escaped his lips. Then, without warning, he released her and stepped backward.

"I'm sorry," he said, trying to catch his breath. His need for her gnawed at him but he pushed it down deep the way he always did. He'd loved his first wife. But somehow loved Jordyn more. A woman whom he'd never known intimately yet felt he understood better than anyone he'd ever met. Someone whom he'd never made love to, except for in his fantasies, yet had shared so much passion with through fleeting glances and, in a weakened state, a few stolen kisses.

Jordyn's skin was pale but her cheeks were flushed and her lips were ripe with his kisses. Her chest heaved as she struggled to regain her composure.

"I'm so sorry Jordyn, but I think you should go."

"What?" She was breathless and stunned. Disbelief and confusion clouded her pretty eyes.

He knew his words pained her in the same way they did him. He reached out to her, his fingers strumming her slender wrist. Delighting in the rapid rhythm of her pulse. "You are…" He swallowed hard. "You are, lovely," he said decidedly. "But we can't do this."

Her eyes burned with disappointed tears. She needed Brody like she needed air to breathe. Yet here he was, denying her again. It wounded her heart and pride that he was apologizing for kissing her. But more than that, the look on his face was more than she could bear. Where there once was only passion and tenderness, she saw something else she couldn't endure. She saw pity.

"So that's it then?" she said, her voice cracking. Her breath was ragged and her heart was beating out of control. She squared her shoulders, prepared to have it out. She was convinced she could win any argument he threw at her.

Brody noted Jordyn's demeanor was very different from the way she'd acted only a few months prior when he'd tried to help and she'd refused to admit she needed it. He recalled their exchange with equal parts sadness and frustration.

"I don't need you to rescue me," she'd told him that day.

"No?" he'd challenged. At that time he'd been angry. But when he'd raised his voice to express his frustration, she'd shrunk away from him. He'd looked on in horror at the way she'd recoiled. It had pained him to realize she'd been terrified. Of him! The hard truth had clawed at his belly and made his blood boil. It was at that moment he'd realized how much he hated Kane. Not out of petty jealousy. But for the way Kane had treated someone as precious as Jordyn. Her pretty, green eyes had been wide with anguish. And fear.

He'd taken a breath, lowered his voice and spoken in a soothing tone.

"I want you to understand something," he'd told her. "I'm pissed. Pissed as hell you won't let me help you. What we're doing right now is having a healthy argument. That means nobody's going to get hurt during it. Understood?"

He'd pulled her gently to him, placing a tender hand on her cheek as he traced her trembling lips with his thumb. But, after sensing he wasn't getting anywhere, he'd pulled back and let her walk away. He'd felt troubled by her refusal of his help, realizing her pride wasn't why she'd refused him. He knew what pride looked like and that wasn't it. It was as if she'd felt she didn't deserve his help. And that pained him most of all.

But the woman who stood before him just then didn't recoil. She stepped towards him, determined and unafraid.

"So that's it then?" she repeated. Her green eyes flashed with fury. Not fear.

His eyes locked with hers. He hated ending things with her before they'd begun. But not as much as he hated the thought of dishonoring her. The thought of doing something he felt she'd regret. He grimaced, feeling the full weight of his decision, and hoping someday she'd understand. "I'm afraid it has to be."

"Fine," she snapped, doing her best to resent him. "If that's what you want. Just don't forget my coming here was your idea in the first place." She straightened her blouse, then snatched her belongings from the kitchen counter. But before she turned to leave, she took a long, drawn-out breath and looked him in the eye. "I guess I shouldn't be angry with you. It's really my fault you're no longer mine."

Brody's eyes narrowed in frustration and confusion. The amazing woman standing before him tugged at his heartstrings and stirred his blood. "Jordyn, I'll always be yours," he confessed. "I'm just smart enough to realize you'll never truly be mine."

His words were like a punch to the gut. On the one hand, they offered hope that he cared for her. But his words also held a finality to them—a proclamation that the two of them could never be.

She blazed with fury. But if she was honest with herself, she'd realize it wasn't him she was infuriated with. She loathed the woman she'd become. Hated that she'd taken something as wonderful as what she'd had with Brody and wished it away. Wished so hard it had become a reality.

"You're wrong," she finally whispered. Then she stormed out the front door, ignoring the apologies that echoed behind her and the agony in Brody's voice.

Brody stood by his front door, too stunned to move. Truth being told, he'd invited Jordyn over in hopes of obtaining information on Kane. His current investigation into Jordyn's husband was stalled and he needed more to make an official arrest. But being so close to her had made him forget all his plans. Instead, he could only think of being near her. And he didn't want to betray her trust by pumping her for information about Kane without her knowledge. He considered himself a man of principles. Then again, when it came to Jordyn, all bets were off.

As Jordyn drove back to the house she shared with Kane, her neck and shoulders felt tight. Dread built in her belly. No matter what care and devotion she poured into decorating the magnificent estate, she knew Masters Manor would never be a home. She'd tried to make the best of it, but she didn't love Kane. His good looks and all his money still couldn't make him half the man Brody was. How did everything become such a mess? If only she'd appreciated what she'd had before it was gone.

Tears streamed down her cheeks as she prayed aloud to God, pleading with him to forgive her, and begging him to restore things to the way they had been. For so long, she'd thought all she wanted was a baby and to leave the small town of Sugarcreek in her rearview mirror. She hadn't realized the value of friendship and small-town charm. And above all that, she hadn't fully recognized or appreciated Brody's unshakeable devotion. She shouldn't have needed a marriage certificate to prove that. She'd been a fool. And she'd realized it much too late.

Chapter Thirty-Four

Jordyn arose early so she wouldn't have to face Kane. She was starting to make a habit of avoiding him. It seemed all they did when they were alone was argue. About his long hours at work. About him not coming home. And that morning she wasn't in the mood to fight. She was, however, in the mood to pull the covers over her head and return to the pleasant dream she'd been having about Brody before she'd awaken to Kane's snoring.

She crept out of bed and tiptoed to the kitchen where Frida was already there, unloading the dishwasher while a fresh pot of coffee brewed. Jordyn wandered to the coffee pot. She grabbed a mug from the cupboard above.

"Do you mind?" Jordyn asked, pointing to the half-brewed pot.

"Not at all."

She pulled out the pot and filled her cup to the brim. Then she took a seat at the island, curled her fingers around the warm mug, and breathed in the steam and smell of the grounds.

"Rough night?" Frida asked.

Jordyn smiled. When she'd first met Frida (for the second time she supposed), her housekeeper was apprehensive about asking any personal questions. She kept things strictly professional. But now the two women had become friends. Jordyn realized she made a habit of befriending anybody who worked for her. She wondered if it said something about her.

"Didn't get much sleep," she finally answered. "Kane came home late..." She trailed off. Although she and Frida could pass as friends, Jordyn also knew it made Frida uncomfortable if she was drawn into any gossip or ill conversations about the man who signed her paychecks. "He works so hard and I don't sleep well without him beside me," she lied.

Frida frowned, and Jordyn could tell her housekeeper knew there wasn't any truth to the last part of her explanation.

"Do you think you could look after Aubrey today?" Jordyn asked. She felt silly asking. It seemed Frida was always looking after Aubrey while Jordyn stood in the background as the odd man out. Odd woman out.

"Of course. It's my job."

She was smiling but tried not to take offense at Frida's statement. As the mother, looking after Aubrey was actually Jordyn's job—not Frida's. But she knew her housekeeper hadn't meant anything by her comment so she offered her a gracious smile.

"Thank you. I just need to run into town on a few errands."

When she got behind the wheel, she breathed a sigh of relief. By the time she pulled out of the drive and passed through the double iron gates, her shoulders were slack and she felt like a huge weight had been lifted from her chest. Masters Manor wasn't the dream she'd once thought it to be. It was more like a nightmare. A nightmare with secrets and bad news at every turn. That mansion wasn't a home. The grand estate and everything inside were merely possessions to Kane. She and Aubrey might as well be bronzed and set on a shelf somewhere.

Jordyn had driven for several minutes before she realized she had no idea where she was going. She didn't actually have errands to run. The truth was, she just needed to run. At least temporarily. She switched on the radio and fumbled through the stations until she found a song that relaxed her. The words didn't make any sense to her, but the pretty melody filled the car and soothed her soul. Without another thought, she headed out of town. She smiled to herself as she passed the sign that read: *Thanks for visiting Sugarcreek. Please come again.*

She wasn't really running away, she reminded herself as the miles stretched on and doubt crept in. She'd be back in time for dinner. Frida would cook it, then give Aubrey a bath. Everything would be taken care of. She wasn't really needed at home anyways, she tried to convince herself as she passed through yet another neighboring town.

She was driving through the third town, barely the size of a postage stamp, when she spotted a sign for a hair salon and an idea popped into her head. She whipped into an empty parking space, climbed out of the car, and walked at a brisk pace towards the inviting entryway of the salon.

"May I help you?" the lady behind the front counter with the purplish-blue hair asked. Jordyn felt a stab of panic that her hair might suffer a similar fate if she let one of the beauticians get a hold of her.

She started to retreat, but then found her courage once again. "I'm hoping you can fit me in for an emergency hair appointment," she said.

The woman stared back at her like she was waiting for the punchline. But Jordyn didn't say anything further. Her jaw was set in a determined line.

"Okay," the woman said slowly. She flipped through her appointment book. "Brittany just had a cancellation for her ten-thirty. Can you wait about fifteen minutes?"

She shrugged. "Sure." Fifteen minutes wasn't anything—but it felt like an eternity to talk herself out of something she knew Kane was not going to like.

Fed up with the platinum blonde hair, Jordyn asked the hairdresser to have her natural chestnut color restored. With the salon being a few towns over, she felt comfortable none of the locals would see her and get word back to Kane. Since she knew so little about him and his triggers, she opted for taking every precaution.

When the hairdresser was finished, she whirled Jordyn around in her chair to see the finished product. Jordyn choked back tears when she saw her own reflection and the restoration of her rich, chestnut coloring. Like Brody, it reminded her of her past life, and it filled her with bittersweet remembrance. Happy recollections, but sadness and longing realizing she may never have that life again.

"Where have you been?" Kane asked when Jordyn finally returned home. He folded his arms and scowled at her. "And what happened to your hair?"

Her chin jutted upwards. "I needed a change," she told him, trying to sound as casual as she could.

His glacial stare made her uneasy. She felt her ears turn pink at his scrutiny.

"You don't like it?" She smoothed her hands through it. "Well, I love it. It feels more like me." Her eyes met his, challenging him. She was tired of walking on eggshells.

"So this is what you do now? Leave your daughter all day with the help so you can parade around town and pamper yourself."

Jordyn seethed at his reprimand. "Where do you get off treating me like a child?"

"You're acting like a child." He took a step towards her.

Placing her hands on her hips, Jordyn spoke as calmly and firmly as she could. "Do you really want to get into how each of us spends our time when we're not at home?"

He glared at her. "Now is not the time," he hissed, his eyes flickering over to Aubrey.

Jordyn took a deep breath, then crouched in front of her little girl. "Sweetie, do you think you can go upstairs and play in your room for a little while?"

Aubrey nodded.

"Okay, go up then. I'll be up in a bit to get you." Jordyn ruffled Aubrey's hair, then kissed her forehead. Though she didn't feel the closeness she imagined she'd feel if she had any memories of carrying her—or raising her—she reckoned her daughter was the one good thing in her new life.

Aubrey headed for the steps, then turned to look at her father.

"Daddy, please don't make Mommy fall down again." Her wide eyes brimmed with tears.

Kane was unmoved by his daughter's display of emotion. "Go to your room, Aubrey," he yelled.

"Kane, you're scaring her," Jordyn said, keeping her tone as calm as she could.

"Go on upstairs honey," she told her. "Mommy will be fine."

Once they were alone, Jordyn expected she and Kane would have it out. But instead he shot her a withering look, then headed for the kitchen to grab his wallet and keys from the counter.

"Going to see Molly?" she asked brazenly, no longer caring what this man did with his time.

"Enjoy breakfast at Brody's the other day?" he shot back.

She was nearly struck dumb at realizing Kane was keeping tabs on her. She wondered if he had people watching her or if he'd simply tracked her phone. She processed this information as she did her best to appear unfazed. She crossed her arms in front of her chest.

"Brody is a friend."

"And Molly's real friendly." He smiled smugly, then walked out the door.

As she watched him go, Jordyn saw Kane clearly now. Saw him for the person he was. She wondered how she could have been so blinded before. His falsetto charm seemed so transparent now. It was as if he'd finally stepped from the alluring shadows and had been found wanting in the harshness of the light.

Chapter Thirty-Five

Jordyn rolled her eyes at the caller I.D. Life in shambles, and only days away from having to share Christmas with a man she could barely stand to look at, the name displayed across her phone was the last person she wanted to talk to.

"What do you want?" she answered, not bothering to mask her irritation.

"Jordyn, it's Molly," the voice on the other end of the line said in a hushed, urgent tone.

"I know who this is," she snapped.

A sob escaped Molly's lips. "I didn't know who else to call," she choked out. Then she burst into tears.

At hearing her cry, Jordyn felt a pang of remorse and pity. Her tone softened. "Molly, what's wrong?"

Silence. Then a sniffling sound.

"Molly?"

"Can you come pick me up?" she asked after a pause.

"Don't you have a car?" Jordyn thought back to Molly's flashy, white SUV she'd been parading around town—realizing for the first time it was likely Kane who'd purchased it for her.

There was another pause. Then a timid utterance of shame. "Kane took my keys and I'm afraid of what he might do if he comes back."

Jordyn swore under her breath. She and Molly really had picked a winner. "I'll be right over."

She sped to Molly's house. Apprehension gnawed in her belly as she gripped the steering wheel. The scorned woman in her wanted to let Molly suffer for the choices she'd made. But she couldn't bring herself to be so calloused. She pulled into the drive and flew up the dilapidated porch steps.

She found Molly sitting on the kitchen floor, her knees pulled to her chest. Broken dishes were scattered around the sagging floor. When Molly looked up, her eyes were red rimmed and her upper lip was puffy.

Jordyn rushed to her side, crouching down next to her. "Molly, what happened?"

A look of guilt swept over Molly's face and her cheeks reddened. "I gave him an ultimatum."

"You what?"

"I'm pregnant," she wailed. "I told him it was you or me."

Jordyn knew she should be furious, but instead all she felt was sorrow. And shame. Shame for the way her husband was acting and that, until recently, she'd been too blind to see him for the person he was. She took a deep breath and spoke calmly. "And I'm guessing that didn't go over well."

Molly buried her head in her hands as her shoulders shook. "He said I have to get rid of the baby. He threatened to ruin me. I was so frightened. I honestly thought he was going to kill me."

With a furrowed brow, Jordyn reached into her purse for her cellphone. "I'm calling the sheriff," she explained.

"No police. Please."

"Brody is a friend," she explained, although she feared after the way she'd left things, her statement may no longer be accurate. "He'll be discreet, but he'll also know what to do."

Molly looked hesitant. More than that, she looked terrified.

"We can trust him," Jordyn reassured her.

"Yeah?" she said, laughing timidly. "Because clearly we're both such good judges of character."

"Sarcasm. I like it," Jordyn grinned. "I didn't know you had it in you."

Brody arrived within minutes. He crossed the room and wrapped Jordyn in a fierce hug, burying his head in her chestnut hair and no longer carrying if the gesture was inappropriate. Damn, he'd missed that hair color. Once he was convinced she was okay, he turned his attention to Molly. Straight away he noticed the fat lip and the bruise surfacing on her right cheek.

"What happened?" he asked as gently as he could. He didn't want it to sound like he was placing blame. So often the victims blamed themselves for the abuse, as if there were any excuse to hit a woman.

"Molly's been shacking up with my husband, got herself pregnant, and tried to offer him an ultimatum," Jordyn spat out. Then she turned to Molly and said, "Did I leave anything out?"

At seeing the crestfallen look on Molly's face, Jordyn softened. "Sorry, that was mean." She stared over at the other woman in her husband's life. The woman who, despite everything, she still couldn't bring herself to hate. "Molly, I'm so sorry. This is not your fault. There's no excuse for how Kane treated you."

A tear slipped down Molly's cheek. "It's okay," she said. "You're being more kind to me than I would be if the situation were reversed."

Jordyn placed a hand on her shoulder. "I don't believe that for a moment. You're a good person. We were both fooled by the same man."

"We need to get out of here as soon as possible," Brody broke in.

"I'm sure Kane won't…" Molly tried to reason.

"Kane's dangerous," he blurted out. "You're not the only domestic violence call I've had to respond to where he's been involved." His eyes darted apologetically to Jordyn's, hoping he wasn't betraying her confidence.

Jordyn looked confused. Then shocked as she recalled Aubrey's sweet plea. *Don't make Mommy fall down again.*

She pressed her fingertips to her forehead as things started to click into place. Kane's disdain for the sheriff. The sympathetic look in Brody's eyes each time she ran into him in town. She longed for the days when all she saw in his eyes was love and adoration.

"How many times?" Jordyn asked.

"How many times, what?" he asked.

"How many times have you had to come to my house?" Her eyes filled with tears of humiliation and regret.

His brow furrowed. "Jordyn, I..."

"How many times?" she demanded.

"You don't remember?"

"I don't remember anything about my life with Kane until about a month ago," she admitted to him for the first time.

He looked puzzled.

"I hit my head or something. Kane said I fell off a stool. Now I'm convinced my head injury was more his doing. Regardless, I don't recall much from before I woke up from that injury."

"I'm sorry," Brody said softly. He considered perhaps it was a blessing. Her forgetting the terrible things Kane had done to her. The cruel things Brody had seen the aftermath of and had been helpless to do anything about.

"Not your fault," she said. "Now stop stalling and tell me. How many times?"

He chose his words carefully. Jordyn had always made excuses for Kane. Always refused to press charges. It took someone less than a man to hit a woman. And considerably less of a man to take someone as lovely as Jordyn and make her feel anything but safe and loved. He stepped closer to her, taking her by the hand and letting his hand linger in hers. His eyes narrowed. Not with pity, but concern.

"Many times," he admitted softly. His chest constricted. He too felt the pain and anguish he imagined she was feeling as he revealed the awful truth. He reached up with his free hand and stroked her cheek. "But even once is too many."

A tear slipped down her cheek as she stared back at Brody in disbelief. It was clear to her now, why Kane had been such an expert at helping her cover her bruise that morning she'd awoken in this unwanted reality.

The truth stung. "And I stayed?" she asked, barely recognizing her strangled voice.

"You stayed for Aubrey," he explained, understanding for the first time as he spoke the words aloud. He glanced over at Molly, then back to Jordyn. He took a step back from the woman he loved, squared his shoulders, and cleared his throat. "I think you should both get out of town. Pack a few things, take Aubrey, and run."

"That seems a bit extreme," Jordyn said.

"Your husband's under investigation for fraud and tax evasion," he snapped. "The D.A.'s also working on making drug trafficking charges stick. Then there's his possible involvement with prostitution."

"I can't believe this," Jordyn said. "I mean, I figured he wasn't the most honest of businessmen but I never would have guessed..." Worried she might fall down, she took a seat on a kitchen stool. Molly sat beside her, patting her hand.

"I had everything, and I wished it all away." Another tear slipped down her cheek. "Brody, I'm so very sorry."

The sheriff remained silent, not sure what she meant. He knelt down beside her. "Jordyn, I'll make sure you and your daughter are safe. But we need to go."

She didn't want to argue with him. It would only worry him. More than that, he was probably right. Running was the smart thing to do. But it wasn't who she was. She needed to face Kane. Head on. She needed to tell him in her own words that it was over. That she was taking Aubrey to start over and he could have everything else. She wanted nothing from him.

She wondered if some day there was a chance she and Brody could be together. Or perhaps she'd have to live with the regret that what was once hers would never be again. Like the carefully selected, elegantly wrapped gifts she gave others every Christmas, the good Lord had seen fit to give her the perfect, beautiful gift in Brody. And she'd exchanged it.

"Jordyn?" Brody's patient voice interrupted her thoughts.

"Yes, sorry," she said. She nodded in agreement. "I'll go." Standing to her feet, she wiped away the tears with the back of her hand. "I just need to use the restroom first."

Her legs wobbled and she felt dizzy; weighed down with remorse and despair. As she made her way to the bathroom, she heard Molly's strained voice followed by Brody's reassuring tone. The hushed tones turned to a roaring sound that echoed off the walls. Her vision blurred and she placed a palm against the paneled walls to steady herself. The shag carpeting swayed beneath her feet, then seemed to float towards her as she felt herself go down and watched her world go dark.

Chapter Thirty-Six

"**Y**ou okay? Jordyn? Jordyn, talk to me." A man's voice penetrated the ringing in her ears.

Jordyn's eyelids fluttered open. She blinked in response to the harsh lighting and sucked in a breath to shield herself against the pain piercing through the base of her skull. She was lying on a concrete floor. As the room came into focus, she noticed she was in the town grange hall and realized it was Kane leaning over her. She tried to sit up, but he gently pushed her back down.

"Easy, easy. I think you fainted and you hit your head pretty hard."

"Yeah, sure I did. Get away from me," she seethed.

"Jordyn, it's me, Kane." He blinked in confusion at the withering look she was giving him.

When she started to respond, she heard another voice coming closer. She craned her neck and saw Brody pushing his way through the crowd.

Kane politely stood to his feet and let Brody take his place by Jordyn's side.

"Jordyn, sweetie, are you okay?" Brody asked as he crouched down next to her.

"Seems like your fiancée fainted," Kane explained. "Perhaps she's just been on her feet too long."

"Thanks Kane, but I can take it from here." Brody's tone was anything but friendly.

Jordyn looked back and forth between the two men. Kane was calling her Brody's fiancée. Brody was calling her *sweetie*. Her throat thickened with emotion. When Brody leaned in closer, she sat up and hugged him tight, basking in his warmth and familiar, virile scent. His powerful arms circled her tiny frame like a blanket of security.

"We're together, right? Everything is okay between us?" she whispered desperately in his ear.

He pulled back gently to study her. His eyes blazed with concern and devotion. "Of course it is, baby. I'm right here. I'm always going to be here."

When he stroked her hair and stared into her eyes, Jordyn wondered how she could have ever doubted he was the one for her. Even if they could never have children. Even if they didn't have a piece of paper from the state of Colorado, sealing them as man and wife, he was far more than she could have ever asked for.

"I love you, Brody," she told him. It was a relief to say those words so freely.

"I love you too, baby." He tucked a strand of her chestnut hair behind her ear and smiled down at her. "Now do you feel well enough to stand?"

Jordyn noticed the crowd around her for the first time. She searched her memories. She recalled being at the bake sale. Remembered running into Kane and Molly and talking about the nursery. Recollected feeling warm and a bit dizzy. Then, her entire reality had changed and she'd found herself married to Kane. She was in disbelief that at first, she'd welcomed the change. She'd looked at it as a second chance. But it was a second chance that had turned into a nightmare. This moment with Brody. This was her second chance.

She stood shakily to her feet and glanced around the room, ignoring the throbbing sensation at the base of her skull. Ordinarily she'd be mortified at fainting in public amongst a crowd of spectators but she was far too grateful about things being back to normal to care.

"Sorry to scare everyone," she said aloud. "I guess I was going for the sympathy vote to sell more cookies."

There was a murmur of laughter from the crowd. Hailie came running over and wrapped her friend in a hug. "You scared me to death," she said, her voice shaking.

Jordyn hugged Hailie back, so grateful to have her in her life. Tears welled up in her eyes, she'd missed her so much. "I know, sorry," she said. "Drama seems to be following me around these past few days."

Hailie laughed, then her eyes narrowed with concern. With her pretty mouth set into a frown, she asked, "You sure everything's okay with you?"

"Absolutely. Things couldn't be better."

When Molly walked over to ensure Jordyn was okay, Jordyn no longer felt annoyance or jealousy toward the woman. For the first time, she felt sympathy. But above that, she felt friendship.

"I'm good, Molly, thanks so much for asking."

"Oh good. You gave us all quite a scare."

Jordyn smiled. "Molly, would you like to meet me for coffee tomorrow morning?" she asked.

Molly's face brightened. "I should like that very much." But the twinkle in her eye faded quickly when Kane stepped forward. He slipped an arm around Molly's waist, steering her in the direction of the door. Jordyn watched the couple walk away, noticing for the first time how Kane's actions were more about control than affection. She wondered how she could have missed it before.

On the way home, Jordyn and Brody rode in contented silence. The couple sat hand in hand with Jordyn's head resting on Brody's broad shoulder while he drove.

When they reached home, Brody hurried out of the car, raced to the passenger side, and opened the door for Jordyn. Taking her by the hand, he helped her out of the vehicle.

"I feel fine," she told him for the hundredth time. "You don't have to handle me so gently. In fact," she teased, raising an eyebrow, "I'd rather you'd didn't."

He smiled wolfishly at her provocative statement. Pulling her close, he kissed her. Hard.

"Well, then let's not waste any time," he said. He placed his hand in hers and all but dragged her into the house.

In the bedroom, he worked quickly to undress her, then himself. Naked and trembling with desire, Jordyn eyed him with eager anticipation as he unbuckled his belt and jerked it free. He yanked off his pants, then slipped out of his shirt and tossed it in the corner next to Jordyn's dress and lacy panties. There was a chill in the air and Brody circled Jordyn's taut nipples with his fingertips. She sucked in a breath as his tongue took over tormenting where his fingers had left off. Her head lulled back and she laced her slender fingers through his thick, wavy hair.

"I love you," she told him, desperate for him to hear it and keenly aware of how much she'd missed having the freedom to tell him.

"I love you, Jordyn. Always and forever."

She burned with passion at hearing the words she'd been longing to hear. She swayed, melting into him. She thought she might sink to the floor if Brody wasn't holding her steady.

They fell together onto the bed as Brody's mouth claimed hers. His naked, muscular body formed perfectly against hers. As he slid inside her, she lifted her hips to meet him. More than ever she needed him to fill her. To feel his love and desire as he took his time with her. Her fingertips explored the sinewed shape of his back as she matched Brody's mounting tempo. She called out his name, begging him to continue. Or to release her. Or both. His strong hands were on her, clasping her wrists. Roving down her thighs. His hands were eager. Greedy. Yet generous and gentle as they brought and sought pleasure. Brody took her higher. Deeper. Their maddening rhythm was headed for an explosion. And just when Jordyn thought she couldn't take anymore, she and Brody rose and fell together, then collapsed in each other's arms.

Afterwards, as they both lay there, sated and bodies slick with exertion, Jordyn again found herself being thankful for the man Brody was. She no longer needed to compare him to Kane. There was no comparison.

The next morning she felt intense relief at awaking in Brody's arms. The mattress wasn't as plush. The thread count of the sheets weren't as high as she'd grown accustomed to. But lying there next to him, it was the most comfortable she'd ever been. She started to snuggle up to him, but then felt a queasiness in her stomach. She bolted out of bed and rushed to the bathroom. Dropping to her knees, she threw up in the toilet.

She started to stand, but dizziness hit her again. Her first thought was that she might faint and wake up back in a world with Kane. She shuddered at the thought as she stumbled to the sink and splashed cold water over her face.

"Babe, you okay?" Brody spoke up from the open doorway.

Her back still turned to him she lifted her eyes to stare at him through the reflection in the mirror. "I'm not sure," she admitted. "I keep having these dizzy spells. Then this morning I just feel so sick." She grabbed the hand towel from the rack and began to dab her clammy skin.

Brody stroked his chin, grinning widely.

"Well, you're in an awfully good mood at witnessing my illness," she said lightly, trying not to be cross with him as she dry-heaved over the sink.

"So, you're feeling sick. In the morning." He arched an eyebrow.

Jordyn turned away from the mirror to face him. "You think…" she said, barely daring to hope. "But I took a test a few days ago…"

"Maybe it was too early," he offered. He tried to keep the hope out of his voice. He wanted this as badly as she did but didn't want to set her up for more disappointment.

Minutes later the pair paced back and forth in front of the bathroom door. Brody checked his pocket watch, stared at the second hand as it slowly ticked away. Thirty seconds remaining. Then fifteen. Then…

"It's time," he said.

Jordyn grabbed his arm. "You check. I don't think I can."

Shoving the watch back into his pocket, he cupped her chin in his hand then softly kissed her lips. "Whatever the result, we have each other." His brow furrowed, praying he'd be enough for her.

"I know," she said. "And that is more than enough for me, really." Tears of love and hope glistened in her green eyes.

"Cover me, I'm going in," he teased, shooting her a nervous grin.

He disappeared behind the bathroom door and Jordyn heard him fumbling around inside. "What's taking so long in there?" she called out impatiently.

"I'm reading the directions," he hollered back.

"Since when do men read directions?"

"What's that?"

Jordyn rolled her eyes, anxious and growing impatient with each passing moment. "How many lines?" she yelled. She had her eyes closed as she silently prayed for a positive result or the strength to get through the disappointment if it was not.

"Open your eyes," Brody said, merely inches away from her.

Her eyes opened and he held up the stick. Through her tears she could make out two pink lines. She blinked twice, trying to make sure she wasn't just seeing double. "We did it," she whispered in disbelief.

"Congratulations, Mama," Brody told her, grinning. She threw her arms around his neck and kissed him over and over. His arms remained limp at his sides, still clutching the stick.

"Aren't you going to hug me, Brody?"

He cleared his throat. "Um, I think I'll wash my hands first." Jordyn burst out laughing as Brody walked back into the bathroom. She heard the sink turn on. Heard him wash, then dry his hands, then waited for him to return to her. When he walked out of the bathroom, his eyes shone with pride and that same look of adoration she would never again take for granted.

When he dropped to one knee, it took Jordyn by surprise.

"It's time to give you a proper proposal to go with that ring," Brody said. He cleared his throat, suddenly nervous. "Jordyn Reilly," he said, his eyes matching the soft plea in his tone. "Will you marry me?"

Tears of joy stung her eyes. "Are you sure? You don't have to, just because...I mean I know how you feel..."

"You're not the only one who has been seeing Dr. Keller. There were issues with my past she helped me work out."

"Really? That's wonderful. But I don't want you to rush..."

"Jordyn, I'm tired of living in the past. I want a future and the only future I can see for myself is one with you in it. I want to marry you." His jaw was set in a determined line as his soulful eyes pleaded for her answer. "I want to call you my wife. I want to celebrate anniversaries. Send out family Christmas cards..."

"Yes," she burst out, interrupting his monologue. "Yes, of course I'll marry you."

Brody stood to his feet and took her in his arms. "Thank the Lord, because I was running out of things to say."

Jordyn grinned. "Family Christmas cards?"

"Well, I mean, if you want," he said hesitantly.

"I would love it. I can just see you, me, and the baby. Matching buffalo plaid pajamas."

Brody made a face, then quickly recovered. "If that's what you want."

Jordyn laughed and her soft eyes went misty. "I want you. I want us. The pajamas can stay with the Sears catalog."

Brody chuckled. "Do they still have Sears catalogs?"

"I feel like you're missing the point."

"The point is, I love you. And I want to make our relationship official in every way possible."

"I can get on board with that," Jordyn said. "I love you too, Brody. So much more than I realized until recently."

Brody stared at her. He'd always been sure how he felt about her but there'd always been a nagging feeling she might not feel the same. But just then all doubts left him and he knew she felt exactly as he did. Whatever had been going on between them. Whatever rough patch they'd been going through, they'd reached the other side victoriously. It was time to leave the past in the past and press forward. Together. He patted Jordyn's flat belly. Just the three of them.

Chapter Thirty-Seven

"**E**verybody in position. We're moving in," Brody spoke into his radio. His team positioned themselves on both sides of the door. One nod from the sheriff and his head deputy used a battering ram to break open the door. The mahogany door splintered and gave way against the weight of the blunt, steel instrument.

From the other side of the door, Kane waited with a cocked pistol in his hand. He'd been so certain he was too smart to get caught. He seethed as he clutched the gun tighter. He hated Brody Kingston. Nose always where it didn't belong. The rotten sheriff should have stayed in San Francisco. Left Kane to run this town the way he was meant to. Kane and the previous sheriff had reached an understanding. Sheriff Lampson looked the other way in exchange for a small percentage of the profits. But the guilt was too much for the old goat, and he eventually chose to retire.

"Get him out of here," Brody said once he'd wrestled the gun out of Kane's hands, slapped on the cuffs, and read him his rights. He felt smug satisfaction. The only thing hindering his joy was thinking about Molly. She had two small children and a baby on the way. She'd be better off. He knew it. She knew it. But it would still be hard.

Molly came to the police station looking like the dutiful wife. She swept through the front doors wearing a red, designer suit and a serene expression. "May I speak with him privately?" she asked Brody.

"Of course. Take your time. We'll just be on the other side of the glass," he assured her.

When she entered the interrogation room, her head was held high. She took a seat across from her husband. He looked arrogant, not yet accepting his defeat.

"What did you do to your hair?" His lips curled in disapproval of the dark auburn she'd reverted to after his incarceration.

Even now, he was trying to control her. Her hair should have been the least of his worries. Ignoring him, Molly pulled some papers from her purse. "I've been going through the paperwork with our lawyers. Now, since you inherited the ranch and surrounding property from your father before we were married, it's not considered a marital asset to be divided equally. But it seems you since transferred the deed into my name only. I assume it was to avoid some sort of seizure of assets if things went awry, but the children and I thank you."

Temper flaring, Kane seethed, "The house and land are mine."

"Doesn't seem so, now does it?" Her lips were painted red to match her suit and her full mouth curved into a thin smile.

"Now you listen to me..." He leaned forward to intimidate her but the tactic didn't work.

"No," she interrupted calmly. "It's your turn to listen to me. I'm done with being under your thumb. You've taught Levi that it's okay to hit, and I won't let that continue."

"Judging by your attitude, I guess you've forgotten just how hard I can hit."

From the other side of the interrogation table he expected her to flinch. But she didn't. Her expression remained unchanged. Instead, she placed her palms on the table and leaned in closer. "I haven't forgotten. But I also haven't forgotten what a coward you are."

Enraged, Kane's hands flew upward, stopping at mid-chest—confined by his shackles. This time Molly did flinch, but only slightly. Then, feeling empowered, a smile spread across her well-glossed lips.

"It's over, Kane. I'm putting as much separation between you and our kids as possible. I won't let Stephanie-Ann grow up thinking a relationship like ours is normal."

"And what would you know about a normal relationship? Without me you're just a discarded piece of trash. Now you're damaged goods. Nobody's going to want you." His face had turned red as a beet but his clenched knuckles were stark white. By this time he was screaming at his wife and a police officer stepped into the room to check on her.

"I'm okay," Molly told the officer. Her tone was even and her expression didn't hold a hint of worry. Then she turned back to Kane.

He was seething. His eyes were almost squinted shut, and his brow was furrowed. It was the look he often got just before he struck her. But this time Molly didn't back down. She didn't flinch. From the other side of the table, shackled and outsmarted, her usually larger than life husband looked so small.

"Someday I will find someone else because I'm worthy. But until that day comes, I don't need anybody to take care of me. I have my children. I have my parents. I don't need you."

She stood to go.

"You can't walk away from me," Kane screamed after her.

But Molly proved him wrong and she did just that. She walked out of the interrogation room and out of his life.

"Thank you," Brody told her once she joined him in his office. "We couldn't have gotten him without you." Marvin had finally come to his senses and was given a plea deal for revealing what he knew about Kane. The mechanic would do minimal prison time as a result. A fact that had made Jordyn happy and absolved some of the guilt she carried. But even Marvin hadn't known the full extent of Kane's crooked business dealings. It had been Molly who'd combed through paperwork and finances to find the hard evidence Brody and his men had needed to secure the arrest warrant.

Nodding, Molly said, "It's Jordyn we should both thank. She helped me see what was right in front of me. All the things I'd been blind to. Once I realized it, I couldn't sit by and do nothing." She let out a ragged breath as her eyes filled with tears. The evidence she'd found of Kane's infidelity, namely with the prostitutes he'd kept under his thumb, had stung more than she'd expected it to.

"He can't hurt you anymore," Brody told her. "Even if he makes bail, we'll be watching him like a hawk."

Instinctively, Molly's hand went to her stomach but she smiled up at him. "We're going to be okay."

"You're a brave woman."

She rolled her eyes and scoffed. "A brave woman would have left him a long time ago."

"No," he corrected her. "You were trying to keep your family together. That's brave too. You're a wonderful mother."

She shook her head, still not believing him. "Kane always said…"

"Forget Kane," Brody interrupted. "He's a liar who didn't deserve you."

When Molly's eyes darted to his, shocked by his outburst, his tone softened and he said, "Hope you don't mind me saying." He shot her a sheepish grin.

She smiled warmly. "I don't mind at all. In fact, I appreciate it."

"What will you do now?"

She smoothed her now auburn hair, happy to be done with the platinum blonde and looking forward to growing it out the way she used to. She threw out the hours of accent reduction exercises her husband had forced her into and let her southern drawl naturally return. Kane always claimed the accent made her sound unintelligent. But upon hearing it restored, she realized it was the first time in years she recognized the sound of her own voice.

"I'm going to sell the ranch," she said. "Go home to Austin. Mr. Davis has agreed to stay on and look after the place until it's sold. I only hope he's not staying out of guilt. The poor man keeps apologizing for not having seen how corrupt and brutal Kane could be. I've tried to explain to him that it's not his fault. Kane was good at only showing the side he wanted people to see."

Molly's voice broke and she paused to dab her eyes with a handkerchief she retrieved from her purse. Then she cleared her throat, and said, "Anyway, Mr. Davis is a sweet man. Tiffany, on the other hand, I was only too happy to dismiss her."

Brody smiled, remembering that Jordyn had more than once mentioned Tiffany's shortcomings as a nanny.

Molly continued. "My parents are flying in tonight to help me get things in order. They're looking forward to spending Christmas with us. To finally becoming close to our grandkids. Kane never really let them..." She trailed off, then forced a smile. "Anyway, that's all in the past. I'm going to be a good mother. And they're going to be great grandparents."

"I agree," Brody told her. "I wish you the best, Mrs. Masters."

"Ms. Hauser, please," she said. "Actually, just Molly. Thank you, Sheriff. I really can't thank you enough." She leaned in and kissed his cheek, leaving a faint lipstick mark.

"Break it up you two," Jordyn spoke up from the doorway behind them.

Brody laughed. Molly spun around, contrite, and ready to apologize. But she smiled when she saw the look of amusement on Jordyn's face.

"I wanted to come make sure you were alright," Jordyn told her. "And to see if you needed anything."

Molly's face split into a wide grin. "That's so kind of you, thank you. But I'm going to be okay."

"I know you will," Jordyn said with confidence before embracing her new friend. "You're going to be more than fine."

Stepping back from the hug, Molly said, "I'm sorry you won't get the chance to finish your beautiful design for the nursery."

"Oh, don't worry about that. Besides, you have your own unique style. Once you get settled, I'm sure you'll design a beautiful nursery for the baby."

The compliment put a smile on Molly's face. She'd secretly always been jealous of Jordyn. Her talents. The life she had with Brody. Brody, who'd swooped in more than once to rescue Molly from Kane even though he knew she would never end up pressing charges. He'd never judged her. Or breathed a word of it to Jordyn. Each time Jordyn came to her house to design a room, Molly would look for signs that she knew about the abuse. That Brody had let it slip somehow. But it was obvious he never did. Molly had developed a crush on him through the years— seeing Brody as her protector, and sadly, Jordyn as her adversary. But now, when she looked at Jordyn, instead of seeing her rival, she saw only a friend.

"Well, if you're ever in Austin…"

"I'll be sure to look you up," Jordyn assured her with a grin.

Molly nodded, then turned to leave.

"I'll walk you out," Brody offered, always the gentleman.

Once he'd seen Molly off and returned to his office, Brody crossed the room to Jordyn. He dipped her low and kissed her lips. His fingertips crept beneath her sweater, skimming her bare skin. Then he pulled her upright, steadying her.

"Mistletoe," he explained in response to Jordyn's wide-eyed look and flushed cheeks.

She glanced up at the ceiling. "I don't see any," she said, out of breath.

"Hmm...strange. I could have sworn I saw some." His handsome face wore a devilish grin. He took Jordyn by the hand, then leaned in closer, whispering in her ear. "You know I've loved you since the moment we met."

She stared up at him, eyes sparkling. "You never told me that."

"Well, I'm telling you now."

She grinned, edging closer to him and hooking her index fingers through his beltloops. "I took one look at you and forgot all about New York. I guess that's when I knew it was love."

He leaned in for another kiss. The woman he loved had come back to him. Whatever had been wrong between them seemed to right itself after her fainting spell at the church bake sale.

When Jordyn closed her eyes, she didn't imagine herself somewhere different or in the arms of someone else. She was perfectly content in the arms of the man she loved—in the town she fully embraced as her home.

"You ready to follow me home then, pretty mama?"

A carefree laugh escaped her lips. "Sheriff Brody, I'm ready to follow you anywhere."

Epilogue

Brody and Jordyn sat cross legged in the living room, beneath the glow of the beautifully lit Christmas tree. They were exchanging gifts in the early morning hours while Brody's mom and two brothers slept soundly a few rooms away. Hailie was due to come over that evening to have Christmas dinner with all of them. She was bringing Tom, much to Jordyn's surprise and matchmaking satisfaction.

"Today couldn't be more perfect," she said. Brody had surprised her with two plane tickets to New York to celebrate their official engagement. She clutched them to her bosom as her eyes welled up with tears of happiness. All along, he'd known her better than she'd realized.

She rested a hand on her stomach, smiling happily to herself. Glancing down at her diamond engagement ring, Jordyn was now over the moon at what it represented. Still the perfect fit but no longer the symbol of a false pretense. Instead, a shining promise of the beautiful life they'd have together. Of the family they'd build together.

Brody scooted closer to her, pulling her into his arms and onto his lap. "You're the best gift of all," he told her.

"Then my gifts must have really sucked this year," she cracked, thinking back on the wooden badge holder she'd made for him and the hunting vest she'd special-ordered as she rested her head against his chest.

Chuckling, Brody said, "Oh, you know I loved them." Then, after a pause. "And they were such a surprise."

She laughed, knowing not to believe the gentle lie he told her every year to spare her feelings. Despite her efforts, somehow, he always knew what he was getting for Christmas.

He tightened his arms around her and gave her a gentle squeeze. "You happy?" he asked, suspecting he already knew the answer.

"Blissfully," Jordyn said with a contented sigh. "You happy?"

"Hmm...What's a more manly word for *blissfully*?"

She turned, hitting him playfully on the shoulder.

Still laughing, he said, "Fine, blissfully it is."

And when his mouth claimed hers, they both knew they'd found their perfect someone.

Gwyneth smiled happily to herself as she folded up the sweater dress Jordyn had given her and packed it carefully into her tattered suitcase. Her weathered hands skimmed across the soft material, appreciating the quality of the fabric. Jordyn had offered it to her without a second thought. Just as she'd offered her a job and true friendship.

When Jordyn had invited her to Christmas dinner, Gwyneth had been touched. She had even considered accepting. But she knew her mission was accomplished and that it was time for her to move on. She had politely declined the invitation and had given her resignation at the store. Jordyn had been disappointed but remained kind—hugging her fiercely and letting her know she had a job whenever she wanted one.

But Gwyneth wouldn't be returning to Sugarcreek. There were other towns, with other, kindhearted souls who could use her help. People who needed a little nudge to make the correct choice that would secure their happiness. Jordyn had finally succeeded in making hers.

The End

Acknowledgements

I started writing *Jordyn's Choice* after hosting my extended family for Christmas. For me, Christmas ended too soon and I wanted to make it last by incorporating the holiday season into my next novel. I love the idea of romance blossoming over the holidays. And I love, love the idea of second chances. A bout with Covid-19 and other unforeseen circumstances delayed the book considerably but eventually I was able to return to, and complete, this project. It was a true labor of love.

I'd like to extend an enormous *thank you* to my friends and family for continuing to be supportive in so many ways—from reading early versions of my books, offering input, coming to book signings, or reaching out to ask about the progress of my current project or simply to provide words of encouragement. A special shout out to my beta readers this time around. *Amber, Craig, Debbie, Kiersten, Melissa, and Ruth*, your candid feedback was invaluable.

And as always, to all the readers—my continued, heartfelt thanks. It is an honor and a pleasure to share my stories with all of you. I sincerely hope you'll enjoy this latest tale, *Jordyn's Choice*.

About the Author

Blake Channels was born in Tri-Cities, Washington where she resides today with her husband and two children. She graduated from Washington State University and is a wife, mother, and finance professional by day and a writer in her heart and soul—and whenever her schedule allows. In addition to writing romance novels, Blake enjoys spending time with family and friends, soaking up the sun, camping, and curling up with a good book.

Books by Blake Channels

(In Order of Date Published)

- Darkened (Romantic Suspense)

- The Comforts (Sci-Fi Romance)

- Ash Fallen (Fantasy Romance)

- Taken by Storm (Novella & Collection of Short Love Stories)

- Jordyn's Choice (Christmas Contemporary Romance)

Visit blakechannels.com to learn more about the author, read her blog, and stay informed about upcoming events and projects.

www.ingramcontent.com/pod-product-compliance
Lightning Source LLC
Chambersburg PA
CBHW030255200626
46816CB00002BA/649